He loathed Christmas. And yet here he was feeling downright merry.

Something was very wrong here.

He was out of his element and he wasn't thinking clearly. It was as simple as that. He hadn't had a vacation in too long. He was getting swept away. Yes, that was it. It had to be. But he had a job to do, a purpose for being here, and he needed to focus. He wasn't here to flirt with the locals or get caught up in…*festive activities*. The sooner he got out of this town and back to his regular life in New York, the better he'd feel.

But even as he processed this reassuring thought, his stomach rolled with uneasiness. He was struggling to convince himself. And that was a problem.

'TWAS THE WEEK BEFORE CHRISTMAS

BY
OLIVIA MILES

All rights reserved including the right of reproduction in whole or in part in any form. This edition is published by arrangement with Harlequin Enterprises II B.V./S.à.r.l. The text of this publication or any part thereof may not be reproduced or transmitted in any form or by any means, electronic or mechanical, including photocopying, recording, storage in an information retrieval system, or otherwise, without the written permission of the publisher.

This book is sold subject to the condition that it shall not, by way of trade or otherwise, be lent, resold, hired out or otherwise circulated without the prior consent of the publisher in any form of binding or cover other than that in which it is published and without a similar condition including this condition being imposed on the subsequent purchaser.

All the characters in this book have no existence outside the imagination of the author, and have no relation whatsoever to anyone bearing the same name or names. They are not even distantly inspired by any individual known or unknown to the author, and all the incidents are pure invention.

MILLS & BOON

First published in Great Britain 2013
by Mills & Boon, an imprint of Harlequin (UK) Limited,
Eton House, 18-24 Paradise Road, Richmond, Surrey TW9 1SR

© Megan Leavell 2013

ISBN: 978 0 263 90169 6

23-1213

Harlequin (UK) policy is to use papers that are natural, renewable and
recyclable products and made from wood grown in sustainable forests. The
logging and manufacturing processes conform to the legal environmental
regulations of the country of origin.

Printed and bound in Spain
by CPI, Barcelona

Olivia Miles lives in Chicago with her husband, young daughter and two ridiculously pampered pups. As a city girl with a fondness for small-town charm, she enjoys incorporating both ways of life into her stories. Not a day goes by that Olivia doesn't feel grateful for being able to pursue her passion, and sometimes she does have to pinch herself when she remembers she's found her own Happily Ever After.

Olivia loves hearing from readers. Visit her website, www.oliviamilesbooks.com.

For my darling little girl, Avery.
May you have a dream, and may you
never stop reaching for it.

Chapter One

"Looks like a storm's about to roll in."

"So I heard," Holly Tate murmured distractedly. Furrowing her brow, she studied the reservation list and then glanced at the hands of the old grandfather clock at the base of the stairs. There was still one guest unaccounted for, and the dining room would be closing in fifteen minutes. Well, she'd have the chef hold a turkey sandwich and a slice of apple pie. She could always send it up to the guest's room upon check-in, just as a courtesy. Exceptional customer service was something she took seriously, and while a few minor complaints were inevitable, The White Barn Inn had yet to receive a bad review on any travel website Holly knew of. The repeat customers she saw year after year—and the referrals they provided—always filled her heart with a sense of pride and warmth.

"They say we should get three or four inches tonight," the assistant manager and housekeeper, Abby Webster, continued. "Steady through the morning and afternoon, but the Nor'easter's expected to hit tomorrow night."

Holly finally glanced out one of the tall, lead-paned windows that framed the front door. Large flakes of snow were falling steadily on the vast stretch of lawn that separated the old mansion from the main road. There would be no sense in asking the handyman to clear the path; it would be covered again in half an hour. It would have to wait until morning.

"We're still waiting on one guest," Holly informed her friend. Though she was Abby's employer, the two women were also good friends. Life at the inn was quiet and occasionally confining, resulting in long days, weekends, and holiday hours. After leaving Boston five years ago to transform the large historic home she had inherited from her grandmother into a bed-and-breakfast, Holly had retained fond memories of riding bikes or lining up at the candy store on Main Street with Abby during her annual summer visits to her grandmother's house in Maple Woods. Having lost touch years before, the friends had picked up where they had left off and grown even closer since.

"Do you want me to stick around until he arrives?" Abby asked halfheartedly.

Holly shook her head. "You go home to that handsome husband of yours," she said. "Besides, I don't want you driving in this kind of weather at night."

"The streets should be plowed by the morning." Abby stifled a yawn and pulled her red wool pea coat off the wrought-iron rack next to the front desk. She shrugged herself into a hand-knitted creamy wool hat and wrapped a matching scarf tightly around her neck. "Don't stay up too late."

"Have a good night," Holly called after Abby, pulling her cardigan tighter around her waist as a cold gust of wind rushed through the open door. The flames that were burning high and steady in the fireplace in the adjacent lobby flickered precariously. Holly wove her way through the oversize sofas and chairs, pausing to plump a pillow and refold a chenille throw, and then added another log from the neatly packed pile at the side of the brick hearth.

She checked her watch again. Ten minutes until the kitchen closed. Stephen, the chef, would be eager to get home, especially in this weather. Inside the dining room, another large fireplace crackled invitingly, casting a warm, golden glow on the four couples hunched over their desserts and savoring the last sips of their red wine. Conversation was low and intimate, and Holly silently crossed the polished floorboards to the kitchen where inside a clattering of pots and pans posed as a sharp contrast to the serenity of the other areas of the inn.

"We've got a straggler," Holly said, grabbing a Christmas cookie from a tray and taking a bite.

"Those are for the guests!" Stephen chided, throwing a white dishtowel over his shoulder.

"You know me." Holly laughed. "I can never resist your gingerbread. Besides, it's only a few weeks out of the year, so I'm entitled. I'll hit the gym in January."

"Sure you will." Stephen smiled, knowing all too well that this was not true. Holly had only been saying this every Christmas season since the inn had officially opened for business four and a half years ago, and she still had every intention of following through—if she ever managed to find the time. Running the inn had become her life and she poured everything she had into doing her job well. There was little time for anything else. Or *anyone* else, as Stephen also liked to point out.

"Do you mind putting together a tray before you go? A turkey sandwich and a slice of pie would be perfect."

"Are we sure this person is even going to make it in to-night?" Stephen pulled a loaf of sourdough from the basket on the counter and began slicing two thick pieces. "It's getting bad out there."

"Maybe not, but even if he's already tired from a long drive, he might want a little something." Holly perused the variety of cookies and plucked a dried-cranberry-and-nut variation off the platter. She took a quick bite, casting a furtive glance in Stephen's direction. *Delicious.* "Besides, this particular gentleman is staying in the Green Room."

"Ah," Stephen said, laying a wedge of cheese on top of a round of heirloom tomato. Every room in the inn was named after the color of its walls, and the Green Room was the best suite in the house, right down to its king-size bed, steam shower and private balcony. Abby liked to joke that it was named the Green Room because it reeked of money, but Holly had chosen the color specifically because of the way the leaves from the trees grazed its third-floor windows in the spring.

"I should go and see if he's arrived yet," she said, dusting the cookie crumbs off her hands. "Thanks again for putting something together."

"No problem," Stephen said. "See you tomorrow afternoon."

Holly retraced her steps to the front lobby, noting with a stir of childish glee the way the holiday lights, wrapped around garland framing each window, glowed like stars in the dimly lit room. Standing just to the left of the massive Christmas tree was a tall man hunched over the thick doormat, stomping the snow off his feet. His slightly wavy brown hair was wet and slick, and the shoulders of his black cashmere coat were dusted with fine white powder. *At last!*

"Welcome to The White Barn Inn," Holly said cheerfully, watching in slight dismay as the melting snow spilled over onto the cherry wood floors. She darted to the small reception desk to grab a rag, and returning quickly to the scene of the crime, she sopped up as much of the icy water as the cloth would hold.

"I'm afraid I've made a bit of a mess."

"Oh, no…it's fine," Holly said easily, still fixated on her task. "Just a little water, no harm done. There." Once satisfied that the damage was under control, she stood to formally introduce herself to the latecomer and found herself face to face with a shockingly handsome man.

"Sorry again." The guest grinned sheepishly, gesturing to the snow melting off his weather-inappropriate shoes. His turquoise eyes flickered with boyish charm.

Holly struggled to compose herself, finally finding her voice. "Good to see you arrived safely. These roads can be treacherous if you aren't used to them."

"No, I'm fine," the man said mildly. He swept a hand through his damp hair and followed her over to the reception desk. "Believe it or not, there's a country boy hiding under this city slicker." His grin widened.

"That makes us opposites, then. I was born and raised in Boston. I've been in Maple Woods for five years now and I'm still terrified of driving in the snow, especially at night." Holly smiled.

"I'm Max, by the way. Max Hamilton. I'm booked for the next two nights. But then, you probably knew that."

Holly accepted Max's hand into her own, alarmed by the chill of his palm. The man must be freezing. "I had an inkling," she said, noticing how his skin warmed slowly from the heat of her own. The subtle intimacy made her feel instantly connected to him. "I'm Holly. Holly Tate."

"Pleased to meet you, Holly Tate."

Sucking in a nervous breath, Holly fished through the drawer for the key to the Green Room, noting the slight quiver in her hands, but happy for a diversion. Finally locating the familiar green keychain, she handed it over to its temporary owner and went through some of the routine information about the inn. The sound of her voice, on autopilot, filled the room, but her attention was on anything but breakfast hours or turndown services.

It had been a long time since she'd had the pleasure of being in the company of a man as attractive as Max Hamilton, and her stomach fluttered as she looked him over. She estimated him to be in his early to mid-thirties—unmarried, she noted with a flip of her heart as he signed the registration book, left-handed, and devilishly handsome. Something about those electric blue eyes and that broad, kind smile made him instantly appealing.

"I'm past check-in, aren't I?" Max looked slightly alarmed at the realization. "I hope they didn't keep you at work on account of me."

Holly took in the friendly twinkle of his eyes and genuine, lopsided grin and felt herself inwardly melt. "Don't worry about it," she said. "And besides, they didn't keep me at work. I own the place."

Something in Max's demeanor shifted and the glint of his eyes turned murky for one quick, telling second. Holly wasn't surprised. No one expected a woman in her late twenties to be the proprietor of this establishment. She was often met with disbelief when she revealed this fact.

"Surprised you, didn't I?" she smirked, coming around the desk.

Max curled his lips into an irresistible smile. "You definitely did," he said.

Max Hamilton wasn't sure what to make of this revelation. What a strange profession for a woman as young as Holly. An *innkeeper*? In this remote little town? He had assumed that the owner of this quaint establishment would be an elderly retired couple, not the sexy young thing that stood before him.

He'd have to rethink his strategy.

"So you own all this?" he asked, gesturing to the lobby and the rooms beyond. It was clear that a lot of attention had gone into the furnishings and decor. The house was built in the colonial style, traditional with white siding and black shutters, but large and substantial. Coming up the main drive, he'd noticed the wreaths hanging from each window by a thick crimson ribbon, the inviting lanterns the hugged the front steps, the pine garland that wrapped the awning posts. Sweeping his gaze over holiday decorations that seemed to fill every inch of the foyer in which they stood, he had to wonder if that red front door had been painted especially for the holiday. Probably, he decided.

"That's right," Holly nodded and then stopped herself suddenly. "Well, almost. My family's been leasing the land for three generations, but I've been saving toward buying it when the lease is up."

Max raised an eyebrow. "That's a pretty substantial investment."

"You'd think so, but not in a small town like this. The Millers were the original owners of the land back in the early nineteen hundreds and the family has stayed in town for the most part. George Miller is the current owner now and he and his wife have no real use for the land, so luckily we've managed to come to an agreement."

"So then you were right the first time you answered my question," Max continued. "You really do own all this."

"Not yet," Holly corrected. "The lease was for ninety-nine years. It was a Christmas gift from my great-grandfather to my great-grandmother. It expires next week."

"And then?"

"And then hopefully everything can be signed and sealed." Holly smiled, bringing a soft blush to her otherwise creamy complexion and a spark to her hazel eyes.

Max shifted his weight from his left foot to his right, unable to match her visible excitement. He grimaced at the water seeping from his black leather loafers onto the polished floorboards. "I'm doing it again," he warned, glancing at Holly from under the hood of his brow.

Holly laughed at his expression, saying, "Oh, I'm being rude…babbling about the history of the inn when you've had such a long trip and probably want to get settled."

She bent down to pick up his luggage, but Max immediately stopped her. "I may be your guest for the evening, but I'm also a gentleman."

Holly's pale cheeks flushed with pleasure and she refused to meet his eye when she said, "I'll show you to your room, then. Follow me."

Gladly, Max thought, fighting off a suggestive smile. He did as he was told and followed her up the winding staircase to the second floor landing, and then up yet another set to the third floor. He couldn't resist taking in the curves of her figure, the slim waist and flare of her hips under her form-fitting black skirt. Her rich, chestnut brown hair brushed her back, swaying slightly against her narrow shoulders, and he traced his gaze down the length of her long legs as she carried herself silently up the red carpet-lined stairs, careful not to disturb guests who, it seemed, had already turned in for the night.

"Here we are!" she announced breathlessly, catching his eye. Max noticed how large and round her pupils were in the dim light, how her hazel eyes had darkened to moss, interrupted by flecks of amber. Her cheeks had a slight rosiness to them, and her lips were wide and tinted with the faintest touch of ruby lip gloss.

"You honestly planned to carry my luggage all this way?" Max grinned and reflexively winked.

Holly bristled and tucked a loose strand of hair behind her ear. For the faintest hint of a second, Max wondered if this was such a good idea, after all.

As a major retail owner and developer, Max and his team had pinpointed Maple Woods as the ideal location for the next major upscale shopping mall in their portfolio. The demographics were strong, and the location roughly half-way between New York and Boston made a compelling argument. He'd driven through Maple Woods and the four neighboring towns three times each in the last two months, and the thirty acres of land housing The White Barn Inn was the best site.

He'd come to Maple Woods tonight with his render-ings in hand, along with substantial market and financial research to back up his pitch, prepared to meet with the planning board and make an offer to the owner of the inn that couldn't be beat. He'd assumed the owner would be a retired couple, happy to trade in long, relentless days of serving others for a life of comfort and financial security.

He had assumed wrong.

The owner of the inn was this bright, cheerful, drop-dead gorgeous creature. And something told him she wasn't going to walk away quietly. The owner of the land, on the other hand, could most likely be bought. There was no way Holly could top his offer, and George Miller would have to be a fool to turn down what Max was prepared to offer him.

Max rolled his luggage to a stop beside an oversize arm-chair near the far window. Looking around the perfectly appointed room with the white trim and soothing sage-green-painted walls, it was becoming increasingly clear that Holly had invested a lot of time and money into what had probably been a very old home in need of substantial work. The inn could hardly be pulling in enough to make her rich. And that only led to one conclusion.

She loved this place. She wasn't going to go down without a fight.

Unless, Max thought, *I manage to convince her otherwise.*

Holly's nerves were getting the better of her. She didn't know what to talk about with Max—his easy charm and sparkling blue eyes disarmed her—and she rapidly ran through the one subject she knew best. Her inn. "Unfortunately, dinner service has already ended, but I went ahead and had the chef make up a turkey sandwich for you. It's quite good, I can promise you that. Freshly baked bread and local produce. We use only free-range poultry. We bring in homemade pies daily, and there's apple on the menu for today if you'd like dessert. If you'd like to go ahead and get settled, I can bring it up to you. Unless…is there anything else you need? Hot tea, perhaps? Cocoa? A glass of wine?"

Stop rambling!

Max's lips twitched but he said nothing. Seemingly entertained by her formal hospitality, his eyes gleamed merrily. Holly had to admit it felt strange to be talking to a guy not that much older than herself in this manner. She wasn't used to having guests like this; her usual weekly crowd consisted of married couples of all ages looking for a quiet and temporary escape from the hustle and bustle of their hectic city life.

Standing alone with him in the Green Room, Holly's eyes were instinctively drawn to the large bed between the two French windows draped in heavy Jacquard fabric. The crisp white duvet was soft and billowy and the feather pillows were plump and inviting. Holly couldn't help but imagine Max later climbing into this very bed, and she suddenly had a strange longing to curl up into it herself. It had been a long day and Max was a welcome surprise.

"Nice bed."

At the sound of Max's voice, Holly snapped her gaze to him, her heart skipping a beat at his heated stare. She quickly composed herself, thinking of something to say about the linens or pillows, and then gave up. A look of naked amusement had taken over Max's blue eyes. His lips curled conspiratorially.

"A glass of wine sounds great, actually," Max finally said, casually changing the subject and releasing Holly from her misery. "Am I allowed to go into the lobby to eat, or do I have to stay in my room?"

Holly took a second to absorb the question, still recovering from her earlier embarrassment, and burst into laughter. Max stood before her in wide-eyed, mock innocence, still bundled in his coat, looking every picture the mischievous school boy just waiting for an opportunity to taunt the teacher.

She really was acting like a prim headmistress. Knowing the other guests were all tucked in for the night, Holly decided she'd had enough of the uptight pleasantries. It was time to go off duty and enjoy the rest of her evening with something other than a good book for a change.

And what better way than with this devastating charmer?

"I'll allow you to come out of your room if you promise to behave," she chided. As soon as she saw Max's surprised reaction, she immediately regretted her words.

He flashed an openly suggestive smile and his eyes smoldered with interest. "And what happens if I don't?"

Rattled, Holly frantically searched for the best way to get the conversation back on track. "Then you'll go to bed hungry."

"I never go to bed hungry," Max said confidently, a

cocky smirk forming at the proclamation. He shrugged out of his coat and flung it on the armchair, his lightweight wool sweater revealing a broad chest and strong arms. "Come on," he said, motioning to the door. "You've made that turkey sandwich sound too good to resist."

Descending the stairs single file, Holly was grateful that there was no chance for Max to see her face, which burned with a mixture of pleasure and humiliation. What had gotten into her? She was a proper businesswoman. This inn was her pride and joy. Maintaining utmost professionalism was something she drilled into every member of the staff, and she herself practiced what she preached. Yet here she was positively *flirting* with her highest paying guest of the night. It was shameful!

As they neared the last landing, Holly took three deep breaths to compose herself, determined not to give in to her growing attraction for her newest guest. But as her foot reached the ground floor and she turned to face him, her heart disobeyed and lurched with excitement.

"I'll just go to the kitchen," she said tightly. "Why don't you go ahead and make yourself comfortable in the lobby, and I'll bring everything over to the coffee table near the fireplace?"

She turned on her heel and headed to the dining room, which she already knew was empty. Often a guest or two would stay downstairs well into the night, reading a book, or lingering over a glass of wine. But not tonight. Tonight it was just Holly and Max.

Holly and Max. Has a nice ring to it.

Just as quickly as the thought formed, Holly pushed it aside. She had to get herself under control. This man was her guest. He was a paying customer in search of hospitality, not a date.

Max was hot on Holly's heels. "I'd rather put myself

to use and help you, if you don't mind. Besides, I've been sitting for the past five hours. The drive from Manhattan took a lot longer than expected and it would be nice to stretch my legs."

Holly's stomach somersaulted as she led them into the kitchen. He wasn't going to let her out of his sight. Not that she minded. Not in the least.

"So what brings you to Maple Woods?" she inquired, glancing behind her.

Max stood in the entry to the kitchen, his broad shoulders filling the door frame in the most manly and thrilling way. Holly was not used to being alone in this room with any man other than Stephen, and that was different. Stephen was five years younger than she and madly in love with his college sweetheart; he was the kid brother she never had. Max, on the other hand, was anything but familiar.

"Oh, just business."

Business in Maple Woods? On December 19? Holly frowned. Few people came to this small town to conduct business, much less the week before Christmas, but she knew better than to press. Max was being overtly vague and he was, after all, her guest. Most likely personal business, she surmised. He probably had a relative in town that he was visiting for the holidays.

From the industrial-size refrigerator, Holly retrieved the sandwich Stephen had made earlier. She placed the chilled plate on the tray and set about cutting a large wedge of pie that was resting on the butcher's block. "Do you think this will be enough?" she asked over her shoulder.

"More than enough, thank you." Max ventured farther into the room and Holly felt her skin tingle. "Now what can I do to help?"

She chuckled nervously. "Oh, just make yourself at home. You're the guest."

"Nonsense," Max said firmly. "I've kept you up late, it's the least I can do. Now tell me. Where do you keep the wine?"

Well, wasn't he smooth? Holly smiled and resigned herself once more to his natural confidence. He had a real knack for taking control of a situation, and she liked that in a man. With any other guest, she would be appalled to even allow them entrance to the kitchen, but Max was right. It was late. No one was around. And besides, she was starting to have fun. More fun than she probably should have under the circumstances.

"The rack is just behind that pantry door. And the glasses are in the cabinet above the sink."

Max strode to the wine rack and casually stuck his hands in his pockets as he perused the selection. After a brief deliberation, he made his choice then crossed the room to the cabinet to fetch a glass. With one hand gripping the stem of a second glass he arched an eyebrow and asked, "Will you be joining me?"

Holly hesitated. He was her guest. A handsome one, but a paying one just the same. She should make a polite excuse. She should leave him to enjoy his evening in peace. But one curl of those magnificent lips was all the encouragement she needed.

She picked up the tray and shrugged with a smile. "Why not?"

"So tell me more about the inn," Max said. He took a hearty bite of the turkey sandwich, noting that Holly was accurate in her description. Turkey sandwiches usually bored him, but this one was a step above the norm. Like everything else in this place, it seemed. "How did you come about running it?"

"This was my grandmother's house, actually." Holly

toyed with the stem of her wine glass and forked a bite of pie from the slice on her plate. "When she passed away a little over five years ago, I inherited it. It was much too big for me to live in and since I don't own the land I wasn't in a position to sell. I had been working in a hotel in Boston as the special events manager at the time, and I knew this place would make a fantastic bed-and-breakfast."

Max nodded, absorbing the information and wondering just what to do with it. Perhaps there was a chance that Holly would be eager to move on with her life. A woman of her age and position would surely want to move back to the city at some point. What kind of life would a small town like Maple Woods hold for her? She didn't appear to have any money of her own other than the revenue from the inn. Max was an astute enough businessman to gauge the earnings of this place, and they were hardly a reason to continue. No, she was running the business for one of two reasons: either she had no other options, which would be great, or because she loved her job.

Max studied her from across the coffee table, noticing the way her rosy, plump lips twisted into a proud smile as she described the renovations that had gone into the house before it could be established as an inn. She gestured with her hands when she talked, underscoring her passion for the place, and despite the trepidation that stirred in his belly, Max couldn't help but smile as he listened.

God, was she gorgeous. Now, sitting across from her in the dimly lit room, he was able to take the time to really look at her properly, and he found her more alluring than he had even first thought. Draped at her shoulders, her hair appeared darker in this light, and an auburn glow was cast on it from the golden flames crackling in the fireplace. Her deep-set eyes were alive and innocent, twinkling with unabashed excitement as she spoke so passionately about everything that had gone into transforming the original property.

"I'm probably boring you," she said with only a slightly apologetic smile.

"Not at all," Max assured her. "It's nice to see a person so accomplished and passionate."

Holly's cheeks burned at the compliment and Max shifted uneasily. It was time to call it a night.

Standing, he heaved a deep, long sigh, but at the sight of Holly standing to collect the plates, his worries shifted to something softer. "Let me."

"No, no," she insisted, brushing away his hand. The plates were already loaded onto the tray and Holly stood straight to lock eyes with his. "Don't worry about it. I have to go by the kitchen anyway to get to my room."

Her room? Max's stomach tightened with realization. The thought of it hadn't even occurred to him, but of course it made sense. Holly lived here. This wasn't just an inn; it was her home.

"I guess this is good night then." She stared at him expectantly, a sweet smile on her lips, which were now the center of Max's focus.

Before he could do anything he would most certainly regret, Max stuck out his hand, accepting Holly's slim palm into his own. He held it there for a moment, watching as her eyes clouded in confusion, deferring to him as her guest, or perhaps, waiting for him to take the lead. He swallowed hard.

"Good night, Holly."

Holly gave a small smile. "Good night, Max."

Reluctantly, he released her small, warm fingers and shoved his hands deep into his pockets. The memory of her touch burned his palm. The fact that he hadn't wanted to release it made his stomach turn with unease. He turned quickly and walked through the lobby to the stairs, which he took two at a time all the way to the third floor, not daring to turn back once.

Downstairs in this giant house, a young, beautiful woman was cleaning up the dishes from the dinner she had thoughtfully planned just for him. She was probably eager to rest up for another day of working hard at a job she loved.

She had no idea that as of Christmas Day, he would be the sole owner of the property, and that by the first week of January, The White Barn Inn would be torn down.

Chapter Two

The dining room was already buzzing with cheerful conversation by eight o'clock the next morning. There was nothing like a dusting of fresh snow to excite even the calmest of her guests, Holly had noticed over the years. With Christmas already in the air, today was no exception.

Holly smoothed her winter-white cashmere sweater at her hips and glanced around the dining room once more. It was silly, she knew, to be so nervous over the thought of seeing a man—and one of her guests at that—but she couldn't deny the quiver that zipped down her spine every time she caught a glimpse of a newcomer through the dining room door. He'd be arriving any minute, she was certain, and the anticipation was starting to gnaw at her. She wasn't quite sure she had ever taken so much time in deciding what to wear to breakfast before, but the little sleep she'd gotten the night before had allowed ample time for hemming and hawing. And primping.

Ridiculous! She scolded herself once more. Max was her guest. A friendly one, yes. A handsome one…absolutely. A charming one… Holly closed her eyes to capture the memory of that lopsided grin. But a guest nonetheless, she reminded herself firmly. And a guest that would be on his way back to the city tomorrow morning.

"Miss Tate."

Holly turned at the sound of her name and smiled pleasantly at the familiar guest from the Blue Room. "What can I do for you, Mrs. Adler?"

"Have you heard any news on the storm, dear?"

Evelyn Adler was one of Holly's favorite guests. She and her husband came twice a year—once in the winter and again in the summer—and Evelyn always requested the Blue Room, claiming it accentuated her eyes. While slightly eccentric, she was well-liked by all members of the staff, and Holly had personally come to see the Adlers as a Christmastime staple.

"I checked the local news this morning," Holly informed her, "and they're still expecting two feet tonight."

"Oh dear." Evelyn's brow creased and her mouth thinned as she turned to look out the window. The snow was falling steadily, coming down in small, persistent flakes, forming a fresh dusting on the white blanket that had accumulated overnight.

Holly felt a flicker of worry as she considered the encroaching storm and the effect it would have on her guests and the Christmas traditions she had put such effort into planning. She did her best to mask the concern and said with forced brightness, "I hope it won't keep you from enjoying some of the activities we have scheduled for the day. Ice skating on the pond, the indoor campfire with s'mores and of course, your favorite—the morning sleigh ride."

Evelyn managed a smile. "I do love a good sleigh ride."

"Wonderful. Just gather in the lobby at nine and be sure to bundle up," Holly said, but her guest had turned her attention away, her sky-blue eyes roaming to the right of Holly's shoulder with sudden interest.

"My dear," Evelyn said as she wrapped a hand around Holly's wrist. "Who is that *man?*"

Holly glanced over her shoulder to see Max standing near the doorway studying the breakfast buffet. Her pulse quickened as her breath caught in her chest. *Pull it together, Holly!*

Turning back to Evelyn, she mustered a fragment of composure. "That's one of our guests, Mrs. Adler."

"I've never seen him before!" Evelyn murmured, her eyes fixed on her subject matter.

Holly suppressed her amusement when she noticed Nelson Adler shake his head slowly over his wife's innocent enough behavior from his vantage point near the hearth. She said to Evelyn, "He just arrived last night."

Evelyn's eyes flashed with curiosity and she darted her gaze back to Holly. "Alone?"

Holly chuckled at the insinuation and, with the hand that wasn't still in Evelyn's determined grip, waved a playful finger at her beloved guest. "Now don't you be getting any ideas into your head, Mrs. Adler."

Evelyn's sharp eyes glistened at the accusation. She opened them wide, innocently explaining, "I'm just saying that if he's alone…and you're alone…well, do the math, dear."

Holly tossed her head back in laughter, noticing with a slight jolt that she had inadvertently caught the attention of Max himself. Lowering her voice, she decided to put a polite end to the topic. "Enjoy your breakfast, Mrs. Adler. And remember, nine o'clock in the lobby for the sleigh ride."

Evelyn reluctantly moved aside, disappointment written all over her face as she pulled her attention away from Max. She glanced back hopefully a few more times as she returned to her table and her eternally patient husband who stared at her over the rim of his reading glasses, shaking his head once more in mock annoyance before burying his nose in the newspaper.

Left on her own again, Holly did her best to ignore the less than subtle gestures Evelyn was making from her corner, which included larger-than-life head nudging in Max's direction and mouthing of the word "adorable" with increasing passion. *As if I need to be told how gorgeous he is,* Holly thought. It was only when Nelson gave his wife a sharp look over the top of his paper that Evelyn lowered her eyes and focused on eating her breakfast.

Drawing a deep breath for courage, Holly squared her shoulders and quickly plotted her next move before turning around and facing Max. She'd have to say hello to him; there was no room for being coy. He was her guest and she would have to treat him as such. He was no different than… well, than Evelyn Adler herself!

"Good morning," Holly said, her voice softer than usual from the sudden tightening in her chest. She forced a shallow breath and smiled up at Max, her heart warming as the corners of his eyes crinkled into a smile.

"Good morning." His voice was deep and smooth, and something in the low tone left her with a sense of suggested intimacy, as if Max felt they were in on some special secret together. Locking her gaze for enough time to make her heart sprint, he finally motioned to the buffet. "This is quite a spread."

Holly exhaled a burst of pent-up air and with a humble shrug said, "Oh, it keeps the guests happy."

"I can see why!" Max grinned, helping himself to a plate. She gazed at the buffet, trying to see it through Max's eyes. Platters of steaming cinnamon French toast, poached apples with vanilla syrup, fluffy scrambled eggs, sliced tomatoes, and crisp asparagus spears were lined side by side on the antique farmhouse table. At the end, tiered trays held fresh buttermilk scones and wild blueberry muffins, as well as several carafes of strong coffee.

"You have quite a talented chef," Max said as he added a scone to his heaping plate.

"I actually do the breakfasts," Holly muttered, averting her eyes and bracing herself for his reaction. She busied herself by straightening a set of napkins as the heat of Max's stare burned her cheeks.

"You *made* all this?"

Holly shifted her gaze to his shocked face. He was looking at her as if she were half-crazy, as she knew he would. It must seem like a lot to take on—a whole lot—but Holly loved it and she would have it no other way.

"I'm an early riser," she explained as the flush of heat crept around the back of her neck. Realizing her excuse was rather lame, she added, "And I like to cook. It's the only time of day I can, since Stephen, our chef, takes over lunch and dinner service."

Max's aquamarine eyes sparked with interest. Speechless, he surveyed the buffet once more with an appraising raise of his brow. "Well, I'm impressed."

Holly smiled to herself at the compliment. She'd been making breakfast for so long, she had stopped thinking of it as anything more than functional. It was an activity she intrinsically enjoyed, and with the number of guests at one time usually being not more than ten or sometimes twelve—and sometimes as few as four, but thankfully, never less than that—she had become a master of preparing meals for a crowd of this size. It *was* arranged nicely, she supposed, and one might go so far as to find it impressive.

Especially a bachelor, she couldn't help but hope.

"Sit wherever you'd like," Holly said. She glanced at a few tables by the window and caught a glimpse of Evelyn Adler watching the interaction with a tickled smile on her lips and a sheen to her eyes that was brighter than the flames in the fireplace. "Maybe this would be a nice spot," she suggested, pointing to a table farther from Evelyn's access.

Max pulled out a chair and sat down as Holly filled his mug with coffee. "If you're around today, we have some festive activities planned," she said.

Max tipped his head. "Festive activities?"

Holly felt her cheeks flush once more, but she bit back the wave of embarrassment she felt when she saw the twinkle in Max's blue eyes. He was messing with her—looking for a reaction—just like the boys on the elementary school playground. Not that she wasn't enjoying the game...too much.

"Everything's detailed on the chalkboard in the lobby," she said as she started to walk back to the kitchen to refill the carafe. Not quite ready to let him out of her sight just yet, she instinctively paused and tilted her head. "Maybe I'll see you later."

Max grinned. "Maybe you will."

What the hell was he doing? Max sampled a forkful of eggs and chewed thoughtfully. *Maybe I'll see you later. Maybe you will.* What was he thinking, carrying on with Holly in this manner? It was completely inappropriate given the circumstances, and yet...he seemed incapable of restraining himself.

Max ripped off a chunk of scone and crammed it into his mouth hungrily. He sighed in defeat. Delicious. Of course. He took another greedy bite and washed it down with a swig

of coffee so smooth and strong he was already hoping for
a refill. He wanted to hate this place, and he was finding
it downright impossible. From the goose down comforter
to the Egyptian cotton sheets to the scented soaps to the
gourmet food to the gorgeous proprietor...there was nothing to dislike about The White Barn Inn.

And that was just a shame.

Max swallowed another bite of his scone and sipped at
his coffee. Allowing his scope to widen, he scanned the
room, noticing an older woman near the window smiling
at him. Unsure of what to do, he gave a tentative smile in
return and to his surprise, the woman winked and gave a
little flutter with her fingers.

Max fought back a smile as he tucked back into his
scrambled eggs. Avoiding the gaze of the silver-haired
woman in the corner, he focused on the other guests, feeling oddly cheered by the soft tinkle of Christmas music
that lent a subtle backdrop to the buzz of the dining room.

What had gotten into him? He loathed Christmas. He
couldn't stand those twinkling lights or the smell of pine.
And yet here he was feeling downright merry.

Something was very wrong here.

He was out of his element and he wasn't thinking clearly,
it was as simple as that. He hadn't had a vacation in too
long. He was getting swept away. Yes, that was it. It had
to be. But he had a job to do, a purpose for being here, and
he needed to focus. He wasn't here to flirt with the locals
or get caught up in...*festive activities*. The sooner he got
out of this town and back to his regular life in New York,
the better he'd feel.

But even as he processed this reassuring thought, his
stomach rolled with uneasiness. He was struggling to convince himself. And that was a problem. A big one.

As he ate, he scanned the business section of the local

newspaper. It was a far cry from the national news he was used to reading—the biggest story, it seemed, was the rebuilding of the town's library, which had apparently been damaged in a fire several months ago. Max leaned into the paper and squinted with concentration as he reread the article more carefully for a second time, his pulse quickening as he realized the importance of the story and the implications it could have on his purpose in Maple Woods.

It was just the leverage he needed.

Sensing that Holly wasn't going to be emerging from the kitchen any time soon—and that it was probably for the best that she didn't—Max folded the paper under his arm and wandered through the lobby, up the stairs and back to his suite. It was early, but he wasn't one to sit around waiting. He'd go into town, feel out the locals, and then make his pitch to the mayor.

But even with his new information, something told him this wasn't going to be as easy as he had previously thought. And Holly was only part of the problem. There were several moving parts that needed to fall into place, and if one of the necessary parties couldn't be swayed—or bought— then the plans for the shopping center would collapse. A year's work down the drain. They'd be back at square one, trolling Connecticut and Massachusetts for a new plot of land for the project and Max already knew from his own research that no other location would do. The few other options he had considered were too small, too far from major highways, or too close to other competing shopping malls. The land that housed The White Barn Inn wasn't just ideal, it was really the only choice. Anything else would be a far second—the profit wouldn't be the same. The chance of securing tenants would be too risky. The sales projections were too shaky. It would cost them...too much to even think about. It was Maple Woods or nothing. He *had* to make it happen.

Shaking off his own misgivings, Max changed into a suit and tie, grabbed his blueprints and thick folder stuffed with financial papers and locked the suite door behind him. Back downstairs, he crossed to the front door and yanked it open. A strong, arctic wind slapped him in the face and he reflexively recoiled and pulled his collar up around his neck.

Only two hours north of Manhattan and he was pathetically ill-prepared. He made a mental note to buy a scarf when he got into town. And some gloves.

"The drive's not clear yet," a familiar voice behind him said. Max turned to face Holly standing in the open doorway, shivering at the cold.

His brow furrowed. "Oh."

"Hank just got in," she explained. "He's going to plow it now."

Max closed the door. *So much for his plans.* "How long will it take?"

Holly's hazel eyes flickered in surprise. "Eager to get away, are you?"

Realizing he'd spoken too sharply, Max offered a smile. "Sorry, I just had some business to take care of in town."

Holly narrowed her stare suspiciously. "We'll have you in town shortly. Doubt anyone's there yet at this hour anyway. Things move a little slower in Maple Woods than they do in the big city."

Max glanced at his watch. She had a point.

"It will probably take about half an hour to clear the drive, so if you want to go sit by the fire, I can have someone bring you a cup of cocoa."

Admitting defeat, Max realized it was hardly a compromise to relax for a bit in the warmth of the inn. A fresh waft of cinnamon filled his senses, bringing a resigned grin to his face. "How about another cup of that coffee instead?"

"Cream?"

"And sugar."

Holly smiled and patted his arm in a reassuring manner. Feeling instantly foolish, Max stomped the snow off his loafers—boots were another purchase he'd need to make—and shrugged out of his coat. Sitting in one of the leather club chairs by the fire, he pulled out some financial projections and studied them.

"You weren't lying when you said you were here on business," Holly observed a few minutes later as she placed a steaming mug of coffee on an end table.

"Bad habit," Max shrugged, quickly closing the folder. "I've got a lot going on back at the office. And I've never been good at sitting around and waiting."

"Or relaxing?" Holly arched an eyebrow.

Max held up his hands and grinned. "I stand accused. Guilty as charged."

Holly tipped her head thoughtfully. "Christmas is only five days away. I would think business would be slowing down."

"Business never slows down. Not for me at least." He stirred the cream in his coffee and noticed the steady stream of guests filing into the lobby. "But then, I guess the same goes for you."

Holly smiled as she turned toward the gathering crowd. With a shrug, she said, "Yep. But I wouldn't have it any other way."

Max dragged in a breath and rubbed the back of his neck. If she kept talking like this, she was going to make things a lot more difficult than he preferred.

He watched Holly retreat to the end of the lobby and fall easily into conversation with a middle-aged couple. She looked nothing short of gorgeous this morning, with her chestnut hair cascading over that creamy sweater that— even from this distance—looked so soft it was practically begging to be touched. Surely a woman as beautiful and sweet as Holly couldn't be without a handful of men lining up and hoping for a date. She'd talked unabashedly about the inn all through their conversation the night before, but she hadn't mentioned if there was someone special in her life. It didn't appear there was, but Max intended to find out just to be sure.

Holly was exactly the kind of woman he imagined him-self marrying—if he ever intended to get married, that is. And he didn't. Marriage didn't work—he'd lived long and hard enough to know that—even if he wished it did. The older he grew, the more he found himself wondering if maybe…but he always came to the same conclusion: nope, not for him. Some memories were too deep. Some facts were just facts.

So no, he didn't have any intention of settling down with Holly, but he wasn't going to let that stop him from getting to know her a little better. And besides, if he managed to win her over, maybe Holly wouldn't think twice about giv-ing up this place and moving to the city herself.

"Drat!"

She'd done it again. Holly grabbed an oven mitt and threw all her upper-body strength into moving the enor-mous stainless-steel pot of hot chocolate to the back burner just before it boiled over. Flicking off the gas to the stove, she grabbed a ladle from the ceramic pitcher on the counter and began filling a dozen red thermoses with the bubbling concoction. She'd managed to save it just in time, and the aroma of freshly melted dark chocolate mixed with heavy cream was heaven for her senses. She—and more often

Stephen—made this treat in batches during the fall and winter seasons, but despite years of practice, she almost always got so busy talking to a guest that the simmering pot would slip her mind. Today that guest had been none other than Max Hamilton. Of course.

Pulling a jar of homemade powdered-sugar-coated marshmallows from a shelf, Holly dared to steal a glance out the window above the sink. The snow was still falling steadily, but it was the threat of more that worried her. She'd overheard more than one guest grumble about the impending storm and the road conditions, and two others who were scheduled to arrive today had cancelled their reservations. With all the energy she'd poured into the holiday week's events, it would be a shame to see none of it come to fruition.

Her heart ached a little when she considered her real concern. She couldn't bear the thought of being alone at Christmas.

"Hello, hello!" Abby burst into the kitchen, all rosy-cheeked and bright-eyed. Snowflakes still spattered her eyelashes and she blinked rapidly to melt them.

"Hey there!" Holly brightened at the sight of her friend, comforted with the knowledge that she could at least spend the holiday with Abby and her husband Pete. She was their token charity case, she liked to joke. But the joke was becoming old. And she herself was becoming tired. Tired of being alone in this world. Tired of watching life pass her by. All she wanted was a family of her own. Was it really too much to ask?

Hard work usually eased the pain and kept her from thinking of how different life could have been and should have been, but Christmas brought a fresh reminder. It was her favorite time of the year, but it would be even more magical if she had someone special to share it with her.

"Um, Holly?"

Holly finished placing a marshmallow in each thermos and found Abby leaning against the counter and staring at her expectantly. "Yes?"

"Who is that *guy?*" Abby practically hissed the last word of her question, and the gleam in her eyes said everything.

"He's our VIP."

"Green Room?"

"Yep." Holly heaved a sigh. It seemed everyone was as smitten with Max as she was. Chances were there were many more women back in New York with the same intentions.

"What do you know about him?" Abby reached for a lid and screwed it on top of a thermos.

"Thanks...I don't know much about him actually. But we did—we did have a nice chat last night. He's very nice."

"Holly!" Abby squealed and did a little dance on the floorboards. "How long were you planning on keeping this from me?"

"It's nothing," Holly said, instantly regretting she had said anything at all. She was building this up to be more than it was. Max was her guest. And he would be leaving tomorrow. *If not sooner,* she thought, turning to the window with a sinking sensation. "He's nice. That's all."

"No, that is not all!" Abby insisted. "And besides, a man like that is not *nice.* Nice is not an appropriate adjective at all."

Holly snorted. "No? Do you have a better term then?"

"Dashing. Dapper. Completely irresistible."

Holly smothered a laugh and shook her head. "Come on," she said, picking up the rattan basket now loaded with the thermoses. "We've got a group eagerly waiting for a sleigh ride and we don't want the hot chocolate getting cold before we're even outside."

Holly pushed through the kitchen door with Abby in tow, crossed through the dining room and ventured into the lobby, where nearly every guest was now gathered in their winter best around the roaring fire, awaiting the morning's activity. Evelyn Adler had bundled herself into a royal-blue coat with a black fur collar and matching hat. Ever the lady of the house, Holly noted with a smile.

She set the basket on a table near the front door and peered out the window for a sign of the stable manager, Rob, and the horse-drawn sleigh. She searched farther out to the white barn at the north end of the estate, finally capturing some movement.

"Are you going on the sleigh ride?" Evelyn had come to stand near Holly.

Holly's shoulders slumped slightly. "Oh, I'd love to, but I should really stay behind and take care of things."

Evelyn cocked her head in Max's direction. "Even if he goes?"

Holly's chest tightened. "I don't think he's able to go, Mrs. Adler, and even if—"

But it was too late. Evelyn had gotten an idea into her head and she wasn't about to let it go. Crossing the room to where Max sat sipping his coffee, Evelyn perched herself on the edge of a footstool and removed her fur hat. She patted her silvering hair, pulled neatly into a low bun, and smiled almost…girlishly.

Holly's eyes darted to Mr. Adler, who was watching his wife from a few feet away with a bemused expression. Holly dared to near Max's chair, half dreading what she braced herself to hear.

"I don't believe we've met." Evelyn thrust a small-boned hand at Max. "Evelyn Adler. This is my husband, Nelson."

"Max Hamilton. A pleasure, Mrs. Adler." He turned to the older man and nodded. "Mr. Adler."

"Oh, call me Evelyn. *Please,*" Evelyn practically cooed.

Holly felt her brow pinch. In all the years she had known Evelyn, she had never been granted the same courtesy.

"Evelyn," Max repeated, his tone laced with amusement.

"Is this your first time at the inn?" Evelyn inquired.

"Indeed it is."

Holly's heart warmed at Max's patience with Evelyn, but she still didn't trust her most loyal guest from taking liberties. Evelyn had made herself very comfortable at The White Barn Inn over the years and, aside from a few formalities she adhered strictly to, she had taken a shining to Holly's personal life over time. Too much so.

"Mrs. Ad—" she attempted as a polite interruption but Evelyn waved her hand dismissively and refused to so much as spare a glance in Holly's direction. Frustrated, Holly began neatly stacking a pile of magazines, making sure she was just within earshot. Evelyn wasn't going to let up, and Holly couldn't resist gleaning as much insight into Max as possible.

"So you're here alone, then," Evelyn was saying now, an edge of mock disappointment in her voice. "Well, a young man as handsome as yourself must have someone special waiting back home!"

Holly cringed but held her breath, hoping to hear Max's reply above the din of the other guests in the lobby.

"Not really," Max said smoothly, and Holly felt a wave of fresh excitement wash over her. She tried to push it aside as quickly as it enveloped her. She failed miserably.

"What a pity!" Evelyn slid her blue eyes over to Holly and gave a pointed stare.

Holly clenched her teeth and wondered if Max was obtuse enough not to see through this meddling. She doubted it. Frantically searching for an excuse to pull Evelyn's attention away from Max, she bolted upright at the jungle of sleigh bells on the drive. "Sleigh's here!"

Evelyn's interest, however, did not waver. "Will you be joining us for the sleigh ride? My husband and I look forward to it every year. So...*romantic*."

Okay, this had gone far enough! Feeling out the situation was one thing. Pushing it was another. "Max," Holly said. "I think that Hank is almost finished plowing the drive. I know you were anxious to get to town."

"Oh, but he might want to go on the sleigh ride, Miss Tate!"

"Miss Tate?" Max flashed Holly a wicked grin.

Bristling, Evelyn remarked, "Of course. What do you call her?"

"Holly."

Evelyn's eyes snapped open. "Oh, I *see*," she said meaningfully, giving Holly a knowing look.

Holly bit back the urge to raise her eyes skyward. If she didn't love Evelyn so much she would throttle her!

"Unfortunately, I won't be able to join you for the sleigh ride today, Evelyn." Max set his coffee mug back on the end table. "I'm afraid I have some business in town to attend to this morning."

Evelyn deflated into her wool coat and pursed her lips. "Pity."

"Come along, Evelyn." Nelson reined in his wife by physically grabbing her at the elbow and then, more tenderly, placing her little hat back on her head. The pair scuttled toward the door to collect their thermoses and then laced fingers as they waited for the sleigh ride to board. Holly felt a sharp pang slice through her chest. She turned to see Max staring at her.

"Sorry about that," Holly said.

Max shook his head. "They're sweet."

"They are. And very loyal, too. In many ways, Evelyn reminds me of my own grandmother." Holly's mind flitted to her childhood memories in this very home. Those were happy times.

"Evelyn?" Max arched a dark eyebrow and his blue eyes gleamed. "You mean *Mrs. Adler,* right?"

Holly gave him a rueful smile. "You sure you don't want to go on the sleigh ride?"

"Nah, I should get into town."

Holly nodded, hoping she masked the disappointment she felt.

Max pushed himself from the chair and buttoned his coat. Holly winced at how inappropriately he was dressed.

"Main Street is just a few miles west, correct?"

"Correct." Noticing the silk tie peeking out from under his dress coat, Holly again pondered the reason for his visit. There was little business in the corporate sense on Main Street. With the exception of a bank, attorney's office and local doctor, only shops and a few dining options lined that stretch. Unless he was here to do something about the library... Now, that was an idea.

"Lunch is at noon?"

"Yes," Holly affirmed. She had the growing sense that he was lingering. Not that she minded, obviously. Max hadn't even left yet and already she was missing him. He was a sight she could get used to around this old house. Easily.

"I'll be back by noon, then," Max said, his eyes still locked with hers.

Breaking free from his hold on her, Holly reached for his empty mug. "Drive safe. It's slick out there."

"See you later," Max said. A devilish grin curled his lips when he added, *"Miss Tate."*

Chapter Three

The long drive to the main road was cleared, but the three-mile drive to the center of town was not. Max squinted through the snow, which was gaining momentum, the wipers doing little to keep the powder from accumulating on the windshield. Maneuvering his rented SUV through the snow banks, Max discovered he had a newfound reason for preferring city life.

It was a welcome reminder. He was becoming too relaxed in Maple Woods. He belonged in the big city; he knew it. He just needed to remember it.

Turning onto Main Street, Max clenched his jaw at the sight. Pine garlands wrapped around every lamppost, sealed with joyful crimson bows. Wreaths hung on the door of every shop. Pristine white snow covered every rooftop. Everything was almost eerily calming and peaceful.

It was like something out of a Norman Rockwell painting. But he would not allow himself to be seduced by its charm.

Pulling to a stop at the address he had jotted down, Max stepped out of the vehicle and paid the meter for the maximum time. He hoped it wouldn't take more than half an hour to convince the mayor of his plan, but if it took all day, so be it. He had no intention of leaving town without that land.

Business was in trouble and it had been for some time. People weren't shopping in malls anymore. They preferred the convenience of online shopping, the gratification of making a purchase in their pajamas at midnight, the thrill of receiving a package with their name on it in the mail five days later. Of Hamilton Properties' existing portfolio, half the centers were struggling. Development initiatives had been placed on hold for two years, but too much man power, time and energy had gone into this project. And big-name retailers were depending on him to get the job done. If he didn't, more than one department store was already threatening to pull out of under-performing centers. Without those anchors, the struggling malls would collapse.

Hamilton Properties had seen three of their competitors file bankruptcy. Only one other remained in business, and they'd already made more than one offer to buy out Hamilton's portfolio. But Max wasn't going down without a fight. He had built this company from the ground up, founding it when he was only twenty-two. It had been a roller-coaster of ups and downs over the years, and lately it had been mostly downhill, but he wasn't ready for the ride to be over. Not yet.

"Max Hamilton to see Mayor Pearson," he said confidently to the friendly woman behind the reception desk.

"Just have a seat, he'll be out shortly. Last-minute phone call and all that." The woman smiled at him as her eyes roamed over his chest, narrowing on his tie. "Not from around these parts, are you?"

Max spared a wry grin. "That obvious?"

"Most folks in Maple Woods don't wear suits and ties. Especially on days like this," she said. Her smile brightened to reveal a dimple when she admitted, "But I like a man in a suit. Always did."

Max nodded and rocked back on his heels, his eyes taking in the miniature Christmas tree on the woman's desk. She'd even hung tiny metallic ornaments on its small, plastic branches. Her sweater had a snowman knitted into it with some sort of textured yarn. Christmas carols bleated softly from the radio on the corner of her desk and at least fifty holiday cards were propped on every filing cabinet, desk, or other surface.

Seems Holly isn't the only one who loves Christmas, he mused.

Max raked his fingers through his hair and stepped away from the desk. It was definitely time to get back to New York.

A set of leather chairs was lined against the wall. Max sat down on the farthest and pulled a magazine from a pile on the coffee table. Absentmindedly flicking through it, his gaze shifted back to the woman at the desk, who was now humming along to some holiday tune, munching on a Christmas cookie and casually directing the computer mouse with her free hand.

"Oh, I'm sorry!" she exclaimed when she felt his stare. She brushed the crumbs from her mouth guiltily. "Did you want a cookie?"

Max held up a hand and gave a tight smile. "No. Thank you."

The woman frowned. "You sure? They're good. Promise. I made them myself."

Max glanced to the mayor's door. "I shouldn't, but thanks again."

He returned his focus to the magazine, feeling anxious and out of place. He shouldn't have worn the suit. It might turn the mayor off; might make him think Max was strolling into town looking to tear things down and take over. It wasn't his intention at all. But it might just look that way.

Max looked back to the receptionist, who was now plucking another cookie from her tin. "Can I ask you a question?"

The woman looked up and beamed, flattered to be asked for an opinion. "Certainly!" she exclaimed, opening her eyes wide.

"Think I should lose the tie?" Max grinned.

The woman's lips pursed in pleasure. "Definitely."

The mayor's office was decoration-free, making it easy for Max to get down to business. He sat down in the seat offered to him and accepted a cup of coffee. Mayor Pearson was an amiable sort with a warm laugh and strong handshake, and Max was immediately put at ease. So long as he didn't come across as some corporate bigwig in from the city looking to stir up trouble, he should be able to have a reasonable conversation with the mayor over what would best serve the town of Maple Woods.

And he knew in his heart that an upscale shopping center on the outskirts of town—on the land that currently housed The White Barn Inn—would be a win-win for everyone.

Everyone except for Holly, that is he thought with a frown.

"It's a stunning rendering," Mayor Pearson said, leaning over the desk to take a closer look at the blueprints. "It doesn't look like the shopping malls I'm used to frequenting."

"We try and design our centers with their location in mind," Max explained. "It's important that the mall have the architectural integrity of the town so that it just sort of...melts in with its surroundings."

The mayor gave the drawing silent consideration before releasing a long, heavy sigh. Relaxing into a high-backed swivel chair behind his desk, he said, "I'll admit that I'm intrigued. That being said, I can't be sure what the planning board will say, and they would ultimately make the decision."

Max nodded. "I understand there are lots of moving parts here, Mayor."

"Of course, there's George Miller to consider. His family has owned that land for longer than I can remember. If he's not willing to sell, my opinion doesn't even matter."

Oh, he'll sell, Max thought. To the mayor he said, "I plan to speak with him as soon as possible. I wanted to give you the courtesy first."

"I appreciate that," the older man said. "And I'd also appreciate if you kept your business here quiet unless things move forward. Maple Woods is a small town, as I'm sure you've noticed, and people around here don't like change very much."

"I'll be discreet," Max promised.

Mayor Pearson tented his fingers. "The financials you have here are very solid and I'm sure you're aware that we lack proper funding needed to re-open the town library, which unfortunately had to be closed until we can repair the structural damage that occurred in a recent fire. The library means a lot to this town—it isn't just a library. It also serves as our community center."

"I heard something about it, yes." The article mentioned that an entire wing had been nearly destroyed—Max understood firsthand the resources an undertaking like that would involve.

"People don't understand why we can't start rebuilding the portion of the building that was damaged and reopen the place. Or why we haven't already done so. It's just not as simple as that." The mayor paused. "As you can imagine, this doesn't bode well for me. Or a re-election."

Max tipped his head with renewed interest. "That's a tough position."

"Very tough. The thing I've learned about being in office is that you can't please everybody. And believe me, if we bring in engineers and construction crews to rebuild that library, someone would be in an uproar that we didn't use the money to build a new wing onto the school."

Max chuckled. "I can assure you that the taxes you would garner from the center would change things for this town."

"Oh, I know it would change things, and that's why I agreed to meet with you. If I might have a day or two to look over these papers, it would help me in making an argument to the planning committee. But I don't plan on saying a word to them unless George Miller agrees to this. I'm already on the hot seat over this library fiasco."

"I'm not sure you're aware of the urgency of the matter. It appears that George Miller plans to transfer the deed of the land to The White Barn Inn as of Christmas day," Max said.

Mayor Pearson widened his eyes. "Ah."

"I could be wrong but I have to assume that the owner of the inn—Holly Tate—might be less than inclined to sell. So you see, I would prefer to get this wrapped up before Christmas. If possible."

"You do realize that Christmas is five days away?"

Max grimaced. "I'm fully aware. I hadn't realized I

would be faced with this situation. I would have acted sooner if I had known."

The mayor lowered his brows. "Do you always do business the Friday before Christmas?"

Max decided not to give the answer to that question. He skirted it by saying, "It's not Christmas yet. It seemed as good a time as any."

"Guess that's why you make the big bucks." Mayor Pearson peered at Max, and for a split second, Max swallowed hard, nervously hooking one leg over the other. His mind drifted to Holly, to the image of her cheerfully bustling about the dining room in that soft creamy sweater and slim charcoal skirt that hugged her curves in all the right places. His stomach rolled a bit with unease.

Finally, the mayor spoke. "A retail establishment of this size will bring revenue to the town. However, it will also change the dynamic. My parting words to you are these. Tread lightly."

Max gritted his teeth and nodded in understanding. Following the mayor's lead, he stood and accepted his firm grip. The meeting was over.

"Let me know when you've talked to George Miller," the mayor said. "Then we'll have a better chat. Right now, my hands are tied. I'm of no use to you yet."

Max nodded once more and turned to the door with the sinking sensation that very little had transpired in the meeting at all. He had the mayor's approval, but it wasn't his decision to make. Max would have to convince George Miller first. And then the planning committee. And if George didn't agree…he'd have to sway Holly.

He couldn't even think about that right now.

"Oh, and one last thing," the mayor said as Max turned the door handle.

Max turned and his pulse skipped. "Yes?"

Mayor Pearson smiled. "Merry Christmas!"

The shops along Main Street had already opened by the time Max marched out of the mayor's building. Pairs of locals scurried along the shoveled sidewalks, ducking in and out of stores, stocking up on supplies before the storm and scrambling with last-minute Christmas shopping.

Max stopped and glanced at a few window displays, all of which were targeted for the holiday, of course. Santa's village in the stationery store. Elves in the children's boutique. If plans for the mall went through, independent shops along this stretch would probably struggle to survive. None of these stores would be able to compete with national retailers, or their competitive prices.

Max sighed, releasing a long ribbon of steam, and paused in front of a store window, noticing that even the bookstore boasted jolly, fuzzy snowmen in its display case.

There was no escaping it. Maple Woods was a town consumed with Christmas.

At least in New York, he could hunker down at the office or his apartment and forget about the festive activities going on around him.

Max felt his mouth slide into a smile in spite of himself. He'd dated many women in New York over the years, but he'd never encountered a girl like Holly before, and certainly none with her zest for the holidays. Although, in fairness, he'd never really dated a woman long enough to be with someone for Christmas.

Max put his blueprints in the trunk of his car and, after checking the meter and realizing that he had used very little of the time he had paid for, he strolled down the sidewalk in search of some basic necessities.

A jungle of bells chimed when he pushed through the

doors to a sporting goods store. He selected some thick wool socks, a scarf, hat and a pair of heavy-duty boots. If today's meeting was any indication of things to come, he wouldn't be leaving Maple Woods anytime soon, and he might as well make himself comfortable for the duration of his stay. He'd assumed he could come into town, meet with the mayor and spend the rest of the day getting a feel for the town before heading out the next morning. Unforeseen complications were never welcome when it came to business. Throw Holly into the mix, and Max had the unsettling sensation that personal complications were equally threatening.

From a neatly folded pile on a display table, he selected three thick sweaters and a pair of corduroy pants and, after a brief hesitation and the memory of that cold, icy wind slicing through his overcoat, he grabbed a down parka from a nearby rack.

"Do you know where I can get a cup of coffee around here?" he asked the clerk as he handed over his credit card.

The kid arched an eyebrow and studied him. "You're not from around here, are you?"

Max shrugged. "Know a good place?"

"There's not much to do in Maple Woods," the kid elaborated, and Max detected a hint of resentment in his tone. Teenagers. "You've got your bar. You've got your pizza parlor. And you've got your diner."

"Just a cup of a coffee will do," Max said patiently.

"Try Lucy's Place."

Max felt a wave of exasperation take hold. "I'm sorry, but I don't know Lucy."

"Lucy's Place. It's the name of the diner." The kid shook his head and hissed out of a breath. "You really aren't from around here."

Max inhaled sharply, but something inside him resonated with this surly kid. He was once like that. Small-town boy with big-city dreams. Desperate to break free and never look back. "Where can I find this Lucy's Place?"

The kid tilted his chin toward the window. "Just across the street."

"Thanks." Max reached for his bag and tucked his wallet back into his pocket.

"Tell Lucy that Bobby Miller sent you," the kid said, managing a tight smile. "She'll take care of you."

Max squinted as sudden realization took hold. Miller. As in George Miller? After a slight hesitation, he nodded his thanks and jogged across the street to the diner as a blast of wind slapped his face, wishing he'd had the sense to have already put on that parka.

Holly's heart flipped at the sight of Max walking into the diner and she paused mid-sentence in surprise. His broad shoulders filled that ridiculous overcoat perfectly, leaving her wishing she could see the fine details of what lay beneath. He stood in the doorway, all at once looking devilishly handsome and slightly bewildered.

Watching her reaction, Lucy Miller whispered over the Formica counter, "Who's that?"

Holly slid her eyes back to her friend. "He's a guest at the inn."

Lucy lifted her head and murmured, "Looks like you've made quite an impression on him."

Holly followed Lucy's gaze back to the front of the room, where Max caught her stare and lit up with an almost relieved smile. He held his hand up and began winding his way through the crowded tables to where Holly was perched at the counter, his athletic frame allowing him to do so with ease.

"Hey," he said, flopping companionably onto the stool beside her.

"Hi," Holly said cautiously, feeling a shiver of excitement at his proximity. "This is a surprise."

"Thought I'd get a quick cup of coffee and check out the town before I went back to the inn."

Lucy took her cue and pulled a ceramic mug off a shelf. She slid it toward Max and gave Holly a fleeting look. Holly pursed her lips and shifted her focus back to Max. "When is your, um, business meeting?"

"Already happened," Max said simply and Holly's heart turned heavy. The meeting was over. His purpose in Maple Woods was finished. He'd be leaving just as quickly as he'd arrived.

He was only booked for two nights but somehow Holly had hoped something would keep him longer. It was a silly thought, she realized now. He had a life to get back to in New York. A life that didn't include her.

She forced a bright smile. "Did it go well?"

Max pulled a noncommittal face. He shrugged. "We'll see."

Holly narrowed her eyes and looked down to her own coffee cup, not sure what to say next. Max liked his privacy, and she wasn't one to pry. If he wanted to share his reasons for being here, he would. But his evasiveness was unnerving and unfamiliar. Maple Woods wasn't a town based on secrets. If you had one, it was bound to come out sooner than later.

Max was a fresh reminder of what her life had been like back in Boston, and she suddenly realized how much she had changed since she'd moved away. And how little she missed her old life. After her parents died, the city had felt vast and empty. Cold. It wasn't until she moved permanently to Maple Woods that she remembered what it felt like to be surrounded by friends and people who genuinely cared enough to let you in, not keep you at arm's reach.

"I thought you'd be busy at the inn all day," Max observed.

"Believe it or not, I do get out," Holly said with a grin. "Abby helps hold down the fort."

"And Abby is?"

"Oh, I suppose you wouldn't have met her yet. She helps run things. Sort of a manager or housekeeper, if you will. But she's also a friend."

Max nodded, his blue gaze locked intensely with hers as if hanging onto her every word. It had been a long time since a man had paid this much attention to her, and Holly felt her nerves flutter under his gaze. Every time their eyes met, her stomach did involuntary somersaults.

The last man who had looked at her with this much interest was Brendan, her last boyfriend in Boston. And look how that had ended, she thought bitterly. But something told her Max was different.

Not that it matters, she thought sadly.

"Here are your pies, hon." Lucy placed a stack of white pie boxes in front of Holly.

Holly lifted the lid of the box on top and stole a peek at the contents. "Oh," she cried. "Apple-cranberry. My favorite."

"That's for the guests," Lucy remarked with a playful smile. She glanced at Max. "You like pie?"

Max shrugged. "I liked the pie I had last night."

"That was Lucy's creation," Holly explained. "She bakes all the pies for the inn. I drop by every morning to pick them up."

"This one keeps me in business," Lucy said.

"I find that hard to believe," Max said, an edge creeping into his once-pleasant tone. He looked around the crowded room. "This place seems to be doing pretty well on its own."

"Eh. At times. But you'd be amazed how many regulars come in, spend a buck-fifty on a cup of coffee and sip refills for two hours. Like Mr. Hawkins over there." She gave a pointed stare to the end of the counter where an older man sat sipping at his mug, the newspaper splayed in front of him. The poor man had been a fixture at the diner ever since his wife had died more than ten years ago. Holly couldn't remember a day she hadn't come in to collect her pies and had not seen him sitting in that very seat. He clearly couldn't bear the thought of being alone.

Makes two of us.

Max raised his eyebrows as he considered Lucy's logic. "Never thought about that. And on that note, I'll take a slice of pie."

A warm glow flowed through Holly at his kind effort. Why couldn't she have met a guy like Max in Maple Woods?

But then, that was the drawback to living in a small town. She couldn't find the right one in Boston. And now she couldn't find the right one here, either. Max seemed like everything she was looking for and more. But of course, he came with a hitch. He was just passing through her life. He wasn't a permanent part of it.

"What's your poison, stranger?" Lucy asked. She pointed to the blackboard on the wall. "We've got pumpkin, apple and pear."

"If apple-cranberry is Holly's favorite flavor, then I think I'll take her up on the recommendation."

Holly bit her lip to hide her smile and locked eyes with Lucy, who had approval stamped all over her face.

"Good answer," Lucy observed. She pulled a fresh pie off a baking rack and cut into it.

"Looks like we'll need a fresh one for the evening crowd," Emily Porter said, coming around the counter. Holly smiled at her friend, who was another familiar face at Lucy's Place.

"I'll get started on that after things quiet down." Emily paused, noticing Max for the first time, and then slid her eyes to Holly, barely suppressing her interest, before she disappeared into the kitchen.

"I worked in a restaurant in college," Max volunteered.

Holly perked up with interest. "So did I! I waited tables."

"You never told me about this," Lucy said, a sly smile creeping at her lips. "How long were you a waitress for?"

"Five hours," Holly admitted. It was such a short but horrifying memory that she often forgot she had ever endured it.

"Five *hours?*" Max guffawed, his bright blue eyes gleaming with amusement. He stared at her, enraptured, and Holly felt the room tilt.

He was just…perfect.

Holly shook her head and closed her eyes, just thinking of her stint as a waitress. "It was awful. I was in college and I needed a part-time job, so I applied to work at this little café. I showed up to work on the first morning and they spent ten minutes showing me how to work the espresso machine—nothing I tried helped me to succeed in foaming that milk."

Lucy nodded. "It's tricky."

"So they—wait, they fired you for not being able to foam milk?" Max's lips twitched in amusement.

"No, it went beyond the milk," Holly said. "They were short-staffed that day and my boss wanted to go golfing. He spent another ten minutes teaching me how to use the cash register—"

"Let me guess?" Max's eyes danced.

Holly gave him a playful swat, wondering for a split second if she had gone too far, but he swatted her right back. Her heart did a little jig. "So I couldn't foam the milk and I could barely use the cash register. I was the only person working aside from the cook and I had to seat people, take their orders, foam the milk, bring the food, take care of the bill, and bus the tables. It was awful. Well, *I* was awful. So awful, that one customer left me two nickels for a tip."

Max's hand was covering his ear-to-ear grin and his eyes were now wide as saucers. A heavy silence was interrupted by a sputtering of laughter and then Max tossed his head back, roaring. Lucy simply shook her head in dismay.

"Two nickels?" Max repeated, when his laughter had died down.

Holly nodded solemnly at the memory. She had never been so mortified. Never felt so ashamed. But looking back, she had to agree it was rather funny.

"I'm sorry. I'm sorry, I shouldn't laugh. But—two nickels?" Max erupted into another wave of laughter and finally composed himself, wiping at his eyes. "And here I was, just beginning to think you were perfect. Now I know you have a fatal flaw. You are a terrible waitress."

Holly's cheeks flushed deep and hot but her pulse kicked up a notch. He thought *she* was perfect. And here she thought it was the other way around.

"I bet you were a good waiter," Lucy said to Max.

Max shrugged and gave a humble grin. "I was better than Holly."

"Hey!" But she wasn't mad. How could she be? He was teasing her, and there was only one reason why boys teased.

"I'm just being honest." His eyes gleamed in merriment. "I mean, you were able to buy some penny candy with your tips and I was able to, well…pay rent."

Holly laughed but silently considered his words. Max

seemed like the type of guy who came from money. Not one who had to earn it. But then, there was a lot about Max she didn't know.

Yet.

"Restaurant work is hard work. There's a lot most folks don't think about until they're in the business," Lucy commented. She handed Max his slice of pie and placed a fork on a fresh napkin. "It's grueling at times. For everyone. Not that I'm complaining. I love this place—don't get me wrong—but it's hard work. And having a little extra cash, especially around the holidays, helps."

Max's mouth thinned. "I'm Max, by the way."

"Lucy. Lucy Miller."

Holly felt Max stiffen in his chair. She scrutinized him sidelong, questioning the reaction.

"I think I might have just met your son—Bobby, is it? Over at the sporting goods shop?"

Lucy chuckled. "So, you've had the pleasure, then? Yes, he's my son."

"Excuse me for asking, but why doesn't he work at the diner instead of the store across the street?"

"He's too cool for it." Lucy pursed her lips. "He used to help out here, but then his buddy got him that job at the sports place. It's a chance for them to hang out and earn some money at the same time. I can't complain since it keeps him out of trouble, but it would be nice to have the family help at the diner. Instead we're paying another classmate of his to help out on weekends."

Holly shook her head and heaved a sigh. Lucy often confided in her about her aggravation with her son's behavior. Bobby wasn't a bad kid. He was just a kid with dreams that extended beyond Maple Woods. "Kids these days."

Lucy tightened the apron strings at her waist. "Who

knows? Maybe he'll grow up one day and take over this place. Hope springs."

Lucy left them to tend to another customer and Holly turned to Max. She patted the pie boxes gingerly, so as to not crush the delicate contents. "I should probably get going."

A wave of possible disappointment shadowed Max's chiseled face and Holly instantly regretted her words. It wouldn't kill her to stick around for a little longer. But then, why bother getting cozier with Max when he was just going to vanish from her life tomorrow?

"You're really going to leave me sitting here all by myself? Why not stay and have another cup of coffee with me?"

She hesitated. "I should probably get back and see if Abby needs any help…"

"Fine, fine, go. But on one condition," Max insisted.

Holly's pulse skipped a beat. She carefully wrapped her scarf around her neck and gathered her stack of pie boxes. "What's that?"

"Give me a rain check?" He regarded her hopefully.

Like she'd even consider saying no.

Chapter Four

After returning to the inn, Holly continued with her normal routine, helping where needed with the lunch service and overseeing any other guest requests. She spotted Max at lunch, sitting at the same table as breakfast, under the heated gaze of Evelyn Adler from across the room. It seemed dear Evelyn's interest hadn't faded through the morning hours, but if Max was aware of her unabashed stare, he'd done a good job of feigning oblivion. Holly had hoped to be able to chat with him before he was through with his meal, but the phone hadn't stopped ringing. Guests slated to arrive in the coming days were inquiring about the weather conditions and yet another had already cancelled their weekend reservation. By the time she made it back to the dining area, Max was already gone.

Holly smiled to herself as she set down the wicker laundry basket outside the linen closet. She folded a soft ivory hand towel and placed it on its appropriate shelf, her mind firmly on Max instead of the task. She had thought her heart would nearly stop when she saw his tall, muscular frame standing in the doorway of Lucy's Place that morning—it was her usual morning stop, and his presence had shaken her routine...in a good way. She had always enjoyed her quick trip into town to pick up a stack of fresh pies and have a cup of coffee with Lucy, but something told her from now on she would always have one eye on that diner door, half expecting him to walk through, looking every bit the strapping, rugged man that had so unexpectedly appeared this morning.

It was deeply unfair that he had to be leaving town tomorrow, Holly thought with a sigh. If not sooner, considering the storm.

"Holly?" From down the hall, Abby's voice called out softly.

Holly felt her spirits perk at the sound of her friend's voice. "Back here! Folding the linens!" she cried with a smile that drooped when she saw Abby's worried expression.

"Don't get upset," Abby said, her normally pleasant tone laced with warning.

Holly stopped folding a pillow case and groaned. "Don't tell me."

"The Dempseys are checking out early."

Holly drew a sharp breath as her heart anchored into her stomach. "Of course they are."

The women exchanged a knowing look that required no other words. This was exactly what Holly had feared. The storm was scaring people away. And she would be all alone for Christmas.

The thought of the house falling dark and silent for Christmas was too unbearable to consider.

"Maybe the storm will blow over," Abby said gently, sensing Holly's distress, but Holly shook her head.

She had never been good at hiding her emotions and with the ache she felt in her chest, she didn't think she could deny her disappointment even if she tried. This was her home. Her family home. A place of so many memories, which she had promised herself she'd keep alive. This house *couldn't* fall dark and silent at Christmas. It had once, only once, and it never would again. She promised herself that.

Her voice caught in her throat when she said, "I doubt it."

She folded another towel and set it on top of the others, the task suddenly feeling useless. The thought of an empty house tonight made her feel weary with dread. She didn't want to spend Christmas alone. And, much as she loved Abby, she didn't want to spend Christmas at Abby's house. She wanted to spend Christmas here at The White Barn Inn, her own home. The one she had spent so much time and energy creating, whose doors she had opened to the public to share.

She was supposed to be spending the holiday with the cheerful buzz of her guests. Just enough company to keep her amused. Just enough work to keep her distracted, preventing her from remembering how truly alone she really was in this big house—and in the world.

And then Max had to stroll into town and remind her of what she was missing. The hope of a future and a family to replace the one she had lost.

For a fleeting second, she wished she had never met him. It was better to fill her life with guests, to keep the companionship constant, than to risk being left alone again.

"Who else?" she asked.

Abby sighed.

"Who else?" Holly repeated, realizing her suspicions were confirmed.

"The Fergusons," Abby said quietly.

"And?" Panic was starting to build and Holly's hands trembled slightly as she pulled a fluffy towel from the laundry basket.

Abby hesitated and then, as if just wanting to get it over with, she blurted, "The Browns are thinking about it."

Holly nodded gravely as she folded the towel. "Thinking about it." After a pause, she ventured, "Anyone else?"

"No," Abby said evenly. "At least not yet."

"Not yet. Exactly my sentiments," Holly said bitterly.

"It's going to be okay, Holly," Abby said firmly. "Pete and I will have you over. You can even spend the night, if you'd like. It could be fun."

Holly's mouth thinned with displeasure and she glared at Abby. "You're giving up pretty quickly."

"Oh, come on, Holly. I didn't mean it like that. I just wanted you to know you can spend the holiday with us if you need to. Or...want to."

"I know, I know. I'm sorry. I'm being silly. I'm just... It's just hard, you know?" Holly said. Tears sprung to her eyes against her will and welled into warm pools. She fanned them away with her fingers but it was no use.

"I know it's hard," Abby said quietly. And she did know, Holly thought. It was some comfort. "You've had a rough time, Holly, and it hasn't been fair. Not fair at all."

Holly nodded and brushed away another hot, thick tear. She'd have to find a way to sneak down to her quarters and clean herself up before she faced what was left of her guests.

"I know you miss them," Abby said. "And I know this time of year is especially tough."

Holly sniffed loudly and squared her shoulders. Enough crying. Wiping away the last of her tears, she blinked rapidly and let out a small laugh. "I'm being ridiculous."

Abby shook her head. "No, you're not."

But Holly couldn't help feeling indulgent. After all, her parents had died six years ago this Christmas.

Max sunk into the thick duvet and powered up his laptop. The inn had internet access, which for some reason surprised him, and he quickly scanned his email for anything new. Predictably, business was slow this week. It seemed everyone else had something—or someone—to fill their time with for the holidays. Everyone but him, anyway.

Max couldn't remember the last time he had celebrated Christmas. Never in all of his adult years, that much was certain. To him, it was nothing more than an excuse to gather with friends. Nothing more. Christmas Day, when everyone was busy with family, Max tended to work, go to a movie, or go for a long jog—anything to distract himself. Anything to make the day feel like nothing more special than any other. But it was hard not to think about what he was missing, hard not to think about that last hope-filled Christmas all those years ago, and the way his world came crashing around him so quickly. To others, Christmas was a time to build new memories. For Max, it was simply a painful reminder of what he didn't have, and he always felt a surge of relief the day after Christmas, when he wouldn't have to deal with it again for another year.

Skimming over his notes, Max then researched the library fire. The little information he found indicated that the cause of the fire had never been determined, but that it was most likely the result of a teenage prank or random accident. The library had been an historical landmark, donated by one of the founding families of the town, and was essentially irreplaceable. The age of the building lent a complication, from what Max could gather, and a structural engineer would be needed to determine the extent of the damage. Then there was the authenticity of the building itself, and the desire to restore it as close to its original form as possible. The cost of this project was monumental for a town of its size, and it appeared there was a lack of wealthy patrons standing around with their purse strings open.

Max considered the predicament for a long moment. He could understand the mayor's position. Being a real estate developer, Max knew how much a project of this size would cost to build. The mayor had a long, expensive road ahead of him and he seemed fully aware of the impossibility of his situation. Max's vision for this mall could jumpstart Maple Woods's sluggish economy and that library project. The taxes collected from the retail sales alone would fuel that development.

He had the mayor's support. That much was clear. Now he just needed George Miller's. The planning committee was something Max would think about later.

A twinge of guilt knotted his stomach when he thought of how friendly Holly was with Lucy Miller. She had mentioned George Miller in passing the night before, but Max had never stopped to consider that she would know them on a personal level. That created a serious obstacle. Holly loved this inn—why would the Millers agree to have it taken it from her? Holly would never forgive them.

Max rubbed his forehead, sensing the first hint of a headache. This project was proving to be far more difficult than he had expected. He didn't have to push it; he could just let it go. He could head back to New York and start the site selection process all over again after the first of the year. Lose most of the department stores he'd come to rely on to anchor his other centers. Throw more money away. Spend more sleepless nights trying to salvage the business he'd built from scratch.

But for what? For a woman he had met only the previous night? As beautiful as she was, even he knew this was foolish thinking. No, he hadn't come this far to back out now. And Max Hamilton was no quitter. He liked Holly. He wanted to get to know her. And he wanted to build this mall, too.

There was a way to have both, and the two were not mutually exclusive.

A knock at the door jolted him from his thoughts and he quickly shut his laptop and shoveled his papers under a pillow. He ran his fingers through his hair and stood, marching to the door with a pounding heart in anticipation of seeing Holly.

With one last deep breath, he pulled open the door, air catching in his lungs when he realized that the person who had come to see him was not Holly at all.

"Hello there, young man." Evelyn Adler stood a good half a foot shorter than Holly would have, and Max lowered his gaze to her.

A smile twitched at the corners of his lips as he peered at the older woman. Brow furrowed in confusion, he said, "Hello, Evelyn. Can I help you with something?"

A little sigh released from Evelyn's mouth and she pushed past him into his suite saying, "Nelson's taking a nap—a good, heavy meal always does it to him. I went down to the lobby to find someone to chat with and I couldn't find you anywhere, so I thought I'd come say hello."

Max watched with a stir of amusement as she made herself at home on a chair near the fireplace. She looked around the room with obvious curiosity, not bothering to hide her interest. Realizing it would be easier to humor her, Max closed the door and took the other seat near the fireplace. "How long does your husband usually nap?" he inquired.

Evelyn shrugged noncommittally. "Oh, it depends. Sometimes an hour…sometimes four."

Max raised his eyebrows but said nothing. His pulse quickened with anxiety when he thought of all the work he had planned to do that afternoon. At the top of his list was a phone call to George Miller. Evelyn was a sweet lady, but time wasn't on his side and he wasn't in Maple Woods to socialize.

Something I should keep in mind when it comes to others under the roof of this old house, he thought wryly.

"As I said," Evelyn continued, patting her hair, "a good meal does it to him every time. And they do have good food here, don't you think?"

Max pulled his thoughts away from Holly. "What? Oh, yes. Very good food."

"We live in Providence," Evelyn said. "Even with all the restaurant options we have there, nothing compares to The White Barn Inn. But then, that Miss Tate certainly has a way of making her guests comfortable."

Max swallowed a smile and dodged the question. "I take it this isn't your first time here?"

"Oh, heavens, no!" Evelyn exclaimed with a wide smile and Max noticed that she had applied a fresh coat of deep red lipstick in an almost garish fashion. "We've been coming here since it opened. This will be our fourth Christmas here."

"Really?" Now that was interesting. Evelyn must know Holly fairly well, then. Despite calling her Miss Tate, he thought with a flicker of humor.

"The first time we came here we were so charmed, we returned again in the winter. We come in the summer for the blueberry picking, you see—the orchards here are simply gorgeous. And then, of course, for Christmas."

"You don't want to be home for Christmas?" It seemed

a strange time to go away, he thought, but then, as someone who didn't celebrate the holiday himself, what did he know? Evelyn lowered her eyes to her small, bony hands that were tightly folded in her lap. "Little point, really. It's just Nelson and me, you see. Everyone else has passed on and…we were never blessed with children."

Max frowned. "I'm sorry to hear that."

Evelyn raised a hand. "It's fine. We're blessed in other ways. Two days after Christmas, we fly down to Florida to spend the rest of winter in Palm Beach. Probably couldn't do that if we were busy taking care of grandkids."

Max offered her a small smile. "No, I suppose you couldn't."

"And Miss Tate does such a wonderful job with the holiday. She has a way of pulling the Christmas spirit out of people."

So I've noticed, Max thought ruefully.

"She's like the daughter I always wanted," Evelyn mused, glancing at him sidelong and holding his stare. Max fought back another smile. Evelyn's matchmaking skills were far from subtle, but entertaining nonetheless. "Pity that I didn't have a son to match her up with."

"Mmm," was all Max could say to that.

"Was your mother lucky enough to have a daughter?"

The questioned formed a knot in his stomach. "I was an only child."

"I bet your mother's hoping for grandchildren soon," Evelyn observed. She stared at him expectantly, as if willing him to just announce impending fatherhood.

"Maybe," he said. He couldn't really say what his mother hoped for anymore. Once, he'd known what all her hopes and dreams were, and he'd foolishly thought he could be a part of them, too.

Max rubbed his jaw. He wondered if she had found a

way to make her dreams come true. If the sacrifices she'd made had been worth it to her.

If she ever thought about him at all.

He forced a smile, brushing aside an image of the last time he had seen his mother. Her absence was his answer. She'd followed her dreams, maybe even fulfilled them. She'd moved on with her life. A life without him in it.

"Will you be spending the holiday with your parents?" Evelyn pressed.

"Nope," Max said simply. He tried to ignore the heaviness that was forming in his chest. Sensing Evelyn's alarm, he said, "They're away."

Not the truth, per se, but not a lie, either. His parents were away. Where they were, he hadn't a clue, but away, yes. They were gone, long gone. Even before they disappeared in the physical sense, they'd always had one foot out the door, searching for escape in one form or another. His dad found it in the bottle, but his mother... Well, she had greater aspirations than caring for an unwanted kid, it seemed.

"Well, then why don't you stay and have Christmas with all of us here at the inn?" Evelyn suggested, her face lighting up at the idea. "Nelson and I would love that. And Holly, too, I'm certain... I mean, *Miss Tate*." She paused. "She's quite pretty, don't you think?"

Max bit the inside of his cheek to keep from laughing. She always found a way of squeezing Holly in, didn't she? Any thoughts he had that Holly might be spoken for romantically had been erased by Evelyn's overt matchmaking when it came to her beloved innkeeper.

"In fact," Evelyn remarked, "she's really far more than pretty. One might even say that Holly is beautiful."

Max chuckled softly but he couldn't deny Evelyn was correct. From her soft hazel eyes flecked with green to her silky chestnut hair and those perfectly full lips, Holly was truly beautiful. Both inside and out, he mused, recalling that dazzling smile that caused her eyes to twinkle.

"Mmm, quite," he said to Evelyn.

Evelyn latched onto his words. "Then you'll stay through the holiday?"

"Unfortunately, I'll need to be getting back to New York before then."

Evelyn's eyebrows knitted with indignation. "Whatever for?"

"Work?"

"No one works on Christmas!" Evelyn said, her agitation building.

"Holly does," Max pointed out.

"Well, that's *different*," Evelyn said petulantly.

"Is it?" Max asked mildly. "How so?"

"Holly loves what she does."

Max shrugged. "So do I," he countered.

Evelyn sighed in exasperation. She was a feisty little thing, and much as she was getting irritated, he could tell she was enjoying herself, too. "It's different. This is Holly's home. And she likes having guests in her home for Christmas. It isn't work to her. It's…an invitation to share the holiday."

A hush fell over the room. Max felt a punch to the gut at the sudden revelation. Evelyn was right. This was Holly's home and she was purposefully filling it with strangers for Christmas.

Where was Holly's real family?

"And then there were five." Holly placed the key to the Orange Room in the drawer and waved sadly as the Browns rolled their luggage through the lobby and out into the cold late afternoon. The Dempseys and Fergusons were already gone, and with the departure of the Browns, that left only the Adlers, the Connellys and, of course, Max.

Abby turned to her. "Anything I can do?"

Holly glanced at the clock. "Has Stephen started dinner prep yet?"

"I could check."

"Thanks. Let him know about the new head count." Holly made a note about the change in reservations. This storm was costing her more than personal company; it was costing her money, too. And with the purchase of the estate only five days away, she wasn't in a position to be taking a financial hit.

By now, every reservation scheduled through the first of the year had called to cancel. Their money had been refunded in full. Those who checked out early were also refunded their money—Holly wouldn't have felt right keeping it from them when some, who were scheduled to leave tomorrow or the day after were simply afraid of not being able to get home in time to spend Christmas with their families. She would hardly feel justified in penalizing them for such a basic desire, even if she had been depending on their stay.

Oh, well. She had the money for the purchase of the property, and anything else would have just been a nice little cushion for getting through the slower months after the holidays. George Miller had agreed to a price that was both comfortable and fair to her. It wasn't a small sum, but it was worth it to know that the property would be hers and that her home could never be taken from her.

She'd already lost enough for one lifetime. She needed to know that some things were there to stay.

"Holly." Dana Connelly swept down the staircase. Holly knew what the woman was going to say before she even spoke. "I'm afraid we're going to have to check out early."

Holly managed a brave smile. The snow hadn't stopped

all afternoon and dusk was fast approaching. "Did you want to try and leave in the morning?" she asked.

"We think it's better to leave as soon as possible. Before the roads get worse. We can be home in two hours if we leave now." She must have sensed Holly's growing disappointment because her rich chocolate eyes softened. "I'm sorry, Holly. But if we wait until the morning, who knows what we'll be waking up to out there."

Holly forced a bright smile, knowing she had no right to feel let down. These people were her customers. They owed her nothing. She was providing them a service, not the other way around. If they wanted to leave early, she shouldn't be making them explain on her behalf.

It was just another aching reminder of how badly she wanted a family of her own. She was trying to fill the void with this playhouse she had created and, while it served its purpose, ultimately she could not depend on her guests for anything more than they were willing to give. They passed in and out of her life with pleasantries and warmth, but they were not permanent fixtures.

Her chest squeezed tight. Max was no different.

"Of course you can't wait until morning," Holly said to Dana. This was the Connellys' third visit to the inn in the last year. She would see them again. But for now, she had to let them go. "This storm is unpredictable and I'd hate for you to miss out on Christmas with your families."

"Well, I don't know about that," Dana said.

"Oh?" Holly pulled up the Connellys' records and changed their bill before sending the file to the printer.

"This year we're having Christmas with my husband's family," Dana continued in a meaningful tone. She locked eyes with Holly and Holly smiled, her first real smile since she'd left Max at the diner.

"I have a feeling you're not too excited about that."

"Oh, to put it mildly," Dana said with a sigh. "Person-ally, I'd rather be snowed in here for the holiday but..."

"But responsibilities beckon?" Holly flashed her a con-spiratorial grin. *Guess that's one thing I don't need to worry about,* she thought, suddenly perking up a bit. In-laws.

Dana leaned in over the desk and hissed, "They never end!"

Holly laughed despite herself, feeling better than she had in hours. "Here's your bill. I didn't charge you for the weekend, of course."

"Oh, let us pay! The cancellation policy says seventy-two hours, doesn't it?"

"No, no," Holly said dismissively. "It's not like I would have filled the room anyway."

Dana lifted her eyes from the invoice. "Is everyone else checking out then, too?"

"Looks that way." Holly sighed.

Dana turned to the window. "It's really unfortunate."

"It is what it is," Holly said blandly, sadness creeping in again.

Dana suddenly smiled. "Well, one good thing has come out of all this for you. Now you won't have to worry about taking care of guests during Christmas!"

Holly managed a brittle smile as Dana ascended the stairs to fetch her husband and their luggage. *If only she knew.*

Deciding it best to tell Stephen they had lost yet another couple for the night, Holly wandered through the dining room and into the kitchen where Stephen and Abby were chopping carrots for the stew.

Holly grabbed a sugar cookie shaped like a star from the tray on the counter and took a bite, ignoring Stephen's arched eyebrow. "The Connellys are leaving."

Abby set down her knife. "What do you think we should do?"

"I honestly don't know," Holly said. "Evelyn and Nelson are still here. And Max." Her heart soared at the thought of him. Just saying his name made her feel close to him, and the image of his rugged face and dazzling blue eyes made her want to be even more close to him.

Stephen finished dicing the carrots and plucked an onion from a wooden bowl on the butcher's block. With an expert hand, he peeled and halved it, and then quickly chopped it into parallel strips. He rotated one half clockwise and ran his knife down the other side. Scraping the pieces from the cutting board to the large pot on the stove he said, "Well, there's enough here to feed twenty. So I guess we'll be having leftovers."

"How are we with supplies?" Abby asked, delicately veering the discussion back to practical matters. "If the storm hits tonight, we want to make sure we have enough to get through."

"We have enough," Stephen replied. He slung a dish towel over his shoulder and turned to Holly, meeting her square in the eye. "But before I keep going with this, you might want to check on the rest of the guests and see if they even plan on sticking around."

"Stephen!" Abby gasped.

Holly stopped her. "No, he's right. I'm being completely unprofessional, and that isn't like me. I'm going to go check on the Adlers and, um, Max. If they want to leave early, they should know they have the option. I'll go now."

Abby held her gaze. "Okay."

With more bravado than she felt, Holly pushed through the kitchen and into the dining room. Her heart plummeted when she saw Evelyn and Nelson standing in the lobby.

"Miss Tate!" Evelyn said sharply when Holly came into view.

"Yes, Mrs. Adler?" Holly asked, though she didn't need any clarification for the purpose of Evelyn's visit to the lobby. Something told her that the couple was not here for the gingerbread house decorating competition that was scheduled to start in—Holly glanced at the grandfather clock—twenty minutes.

"I'm so sorry, dear, but I think we might need to leave early."

"But—" Holly wanted to ask what better plans Evelyn could have for Christmas but managed to stop herself in time. She really was losing sight of her hospitality today, wasn't she?

But Evelyn and Holly had known each other long enough to understand the unspoken. Evelyn's watery blue eyes drooped at Holly's distress. When the older woman reached over to touch her hand, Holly had to fight to hold back the tears that were threatening to form. She swallowed a painful lump in her throat.

"You know how much it means to me to spend Christmas at The White Barn Inn," Evelyn said. "But we're supposed to be going to Florida two days after Christmas. And if we get stuck…"

Holly nodded briskly, not daring to speak for fear of choking on her own words.

"Oh, I'm torn, Miss Tate! The tree lighting is tonight, and I bought a new hat especially for the occasion. Red with black faux fur…" Evelyn glanced around the room in agony, wrestling with her own emotions. "The thought of leaving all this—" She swept her arm around the room, gesturing to the twinkling Christmas tree, the stockings hanging from the mantel, the mistletoe sprigs under every doorway and the garland framing the windows.

It was Holly's turn to comfort Evelyn. She squeezed the woman's hand tight, realizing how small and frail it seemed in her own. "It will all be here next year, Mrs. Adler."

Evelyn's worried eyes clasped with Holly's. "You're sure, dear?"

Holly smiled warmly. "Of course I'm sure."

Evelyn searched Holly's face, her gaze unrelenting until her fear had subsided. Shaking slightly, she let go of Holly's hand and turned to her husband. "Okay then," she said. "I guess we should go."

"It's the smart thing to do, Evelyn," Nelson said kindly.

"He's right," Holly mustered even though she wanted to cry out and beg them to stay through the rest of the week. "Getting home safely is most important. Do it for me, Mrs. Adler."

Evelyn pinched her lips and wiped away a tear. "Has everyone else decided to leave as well?"

Holly opened her mouth to respond when her attention was suddenly pulled to the edge of the room, where Max was sauntering down the stairs into the foyer, a pleasant expression on his handsome face. Evelyn turned to follow her gaze, her mood immediately brightening.

"Well hello again, young man!" she cooed, clasping her hands in unabashed joy.

Max stifled a smile as his cheeks grew pink. Holly herself could barely keep from laughing at Evelyn's reaction to his arrival, but a bigger part of her felt nearly sick with dread. The thought of Max leaving the inn tonight was a reality that she wasn't ready to accept. The chances of a man like him passing through her inn again were slim to none.

"Max and I had a lovely chat this afternoon," Evelyn beamed.

Holly lifted an eyebrow and smiled slyly at Max. "Oh?"

"Ah, yes. Evelyn did me the honor of stopping by my

room today," Max informed her, his blue eyes dancing with mischief.

Holly bit her lip. She didn't even want to think about what might have been said during that conversation.

"We were just telling Miss Tate that we sadly have to leave early," Evelyn explained and Holly felt a stab in the chest like she was hearing the words for the first time. "Will you be checking out early as well?"

Holly held her breath and the room went still as she waited for his response. She didn't dare look at him for fear he would see the anguish in her eyes.

"I think I'll stick around, actually," Max said easily and Holly's heart rate quickened. She hadn't seen that coming.

Evelyn could barely suppress her vicarious glee. "How lovely!" she exclaimed, fixing her large bright eyes on Holly in a less than subtle fashion.

Holly bit the inside of her cheeks to keep from laughing and Max's eyes twinkled ferociously. The fact that he was just as in tune with Evelyn's matchmaking as she was didn't bother her anymore. If anything, the private joke they now shared only made her feel more bonded to him than ever. A hidden secret was shared between them, lost on sweet Evelyn.

"I was actually coming down to see if I could extend my reservation," he said when he had collected himself.

Extend? Holly still couldn't believe her good fortune. Why on earth Max was deciding to stay longer as opposed to leaving early was beyond her understanding, but she wasn't going to question it. "Of course," she said, regaining her composure. She forced herself back into a professional role, but in the company of her favorite guests, it somehow felt unnecessary. "How long will you be needing the room for?"

"Until Christmas Day."

Holly paled. Five more nights. "Christmas Day?"

Max scrutinized her reaction. "If that's okay. I can move rooms if mine has been reserved."

Holly cleared her throat, refusing to so much as glance at Evelyn, who she could see from the corner of her eye was radiant with joy, her palm placed dramatically on her heart. "No, it's fine. Your room is free. In fact, all the rooms are free, actually."

Max spared her a quizzical look. "All the rooms?"

"We're not the only ones heading out early," Evelyn said. She rubbed her hands together as the plan was hatched. "So it looks like it will be just the two of you in this big, beautiful house!"

Holly watched as Max's eyes widened and quickly darted to hers, searching for verification. On instinct, Holly lowered her gaze, unable to look at him in that moment. Her pulse raced as her chest rose and fell with each breath. Alone in the house with Max. How would he feel about that?

"I take it that dinner has been cancelled for tonight?" Max asked, breaking the awkward silence. When Holly nodded, he suggested, "Perfect. Then you can take me up on my earlier rain check. Maybe you can show me the town tonight."

"But the roads!" Evelyn said.

Max shrugged. "The storm hasn't hit yet. By the time it does, we'll be all tucked into bed, safe and sound." He turned to Holly and grinned. "What do you say, Holly?"

Holly glanced from Max to Evelyn, whose expression was frozen in anticipation. "I'd love to," she said easily.

With that settled, Evelyn released a long sigh of content. "We should get going," she said and Nelson took his cue to take the bags out to the car.

"It was a true pleasure meeting you, Evelyn." Max

smiled down at her warmly and more awkwardly reached in for a hug.

Breaking free, Evelyn giggled like a schoolgirl and Holly noticed her cheeks were stained with pleasure. Holly shook her head, unable to suppress the contagious energy that Evelyn carried with her. "Drive safely, Mrs. Adler. And Merry Christmas," she said.

Holly pulled her in for a hug and only released her when Nelson called from the doorway that the car was ready. Evelyn slid her sharp blue eyes to Holly before joining her husband. "You have fun, dear," she purred.

Holly felt her cheeks color. She had a feeling she would do just that.

Chapter Five

Holly walked back to the kitchen as though floating on
air, completely unable to banish her smile. As much as her
heart ached that Evelyn and Nelson had left, she couldn't
deny the glee that was building with each passing second
at the thought of five whole nights with Max. Alone.

"Dinner is off!" she announced to Stephen and Abby.
They both froze midaction in their tasks, their expressions
transforming from concern to bewilderment.

"The Adlers are leaving?" Abby asked slowly.

"Already left." Holly shrugged. Giddily, she all but
hopped over to the cookie tray and reached for a piece of
fudge before stopping herself. She was about to spend a
week with the most gorgeous man she had ever met. An
image of the way his broad shoulders strained against the
confines of his sweater filled her mind and she snatched
her hand back. Now was not the time to be indulging in

sweets. Now was the time to be indulging in something altogether better.

Get a grip, Holly! He was still her guest. Why was she having so much trouble remembering this?

"The Adlers already left?" Abby cried in disbelief and Holly nodded her head cheerfully. It was sad, yes, but in light of the other news... "Then why are you smiling like that?"

Holly reflexively frowned. "Am I?" she inquired. Stephen shook his head and began cleaning up while Abby stepped away from the counter, her face pale with concern and her eyes wide with something close to fear.

"I'm seriously getting worried about you now, Holly," she said gravely.

Holly smiled as Abby silently followed her back to her quarters, and only once the door was firmly closed behind her did she triumphantly proclaim, "Max invited me to dinner tonight. Even better? He extended his stay. For five more nights."

"He's staying through the *week?*" Abby's eyes flew open in shock and she threw herself down on Holly's bed and stared at the ceiling in disbelief.

"Yep." Holly leaned into the antique ivory-framed mirror above her dressing table and massaged a dollop of moisturizer under her eyes. She looked tired and stressed from the events of the day, but it was nothing a little makeup wouldn't fix. "Until Christmas Day."

"Really?"

"That's what he said." A surge of fresh glee washed over Holly's insides. Five more days with Max. Anything could happen in that time period.

Abby rolled onto her side and tucked her feet behind her. She propped herself up by an elbow and cupped her head in her hand. "But why did he decide to stay longer?"

Holly stared at Abby's reflection. She wondered the same thing herself. The mysterious nature of his visit was certainly odd. "He says he's here on business. That's all I know."

"Business?" Abby scoffed. "In Maple Woods? Over the holidays?"

Holly frowned and considered her friend's words. "It is strange. Isn't it?"

Abby was incredulous. "Strange? Uh, yes! Just a little. He didn't say what kind of business?"

Holly shrugged. "He didn't elaborate."

Abby pushed herself up to a sitting position dangled her legs over the side of the four-poster bed. "Well, it doesn't matter. Business is boring. Besides," she said, coming to join Holly in the mirror, "you can find out all the details tonight. On your date."

A flutter of nerves caught hold of Holly's stomach at the term. Date. Was that really what it was? It seemed so unlikely when she stopped to think of it—he must have an entire life in New York, so what more could he want with her than a friendly face to keep him company while he was in town? Yes, they got along, and yes, he seemed to like her. But liking someone took many forms, and with someone as gorgeous as Max Hamilton…well, chances were he wasn't often without equally beautiful female companionship. There must have been many girls who fell under Max's spell. Holly would be foolish to think she was the only one who could sense this magnetism.

Her stomach churned. A guy like Max probably had his pick when it came to pretty girls. And she was hardly exceptional. Nothing glamorous. Not rich. A plain Jane, in many ways.

She had to brace herself for disappointment. Max's intentions—on every level—were a mystery to her. Getting swept up in romantic notions would only result in heart-break and tears if the evening turned out to be nothing but platonic, albeit pleasant. She couldn't go giving her heart to a man who would rather peruse a spreadsheet than listen to what she had to say. She'd promised herself after her last failed relationship that the next man she allowed herself to develop feelings for would at least have the same priorities as she did.

Maybe Max wasn't so different from Brendan, after all. Despite his friendliness, he seemed a lot more interested in whatever business he had going on over Christmas than the spirit of the holiday itself.

"Why are you frowning?" Abby eyed her through the mirror.

"What? Oh…I wasn't frowning." Holly forced herself back to her surroundings and dabbed some gloss on her lips.

"Don't tell me you're thinking about Brendan."

Holly didn't dare admit the truth. Something told her the night ahead was going be both spontaneous and romantic, and she pushed back the wary hunch that threatened to disturb the chance of hope that was playing out in her mind. It was hard not to think about Brendan sometimes—he'd let her down when she needed someone the most, destroying any hope of a brighter future, when hope was all she'd been clinging to. She hadn't dated anyone seriously since then. And the thought of going into town with Max tonight, while thrilling, was also a little terrifying. The entire concept was so far out of Holly's normal routine that she struggled to grasp the logistics of what a real date would require.

"I'm not thinking about Brendan," she said firmly. And she wasn't. She was thinking about Max.

"Good, because all you should be thinking about right now is what you're going to wear on your date."

"It's not a date!" But even as she protested, Holly couldn't resist the warm glow that filled her.

"Then what would you call it?"

Holly considered the question. "Companionship."

Abby chortled. "Oh, please. A man like that does not need companionship."

"What does he need then?"

Abby pulled a face. "I think you already know the answer to that one. Believe me, there's only one reason that man is hanging around you so much, and it isn't because he's looking for a friend."

Holly bit her lip and considered Abby's point. And hoped to God she was right. She studied her reflection in the mirror and smiled with anticipation. She hadn't felt this nervous or alive in longer than she could remember, and her heart was hammering with possibilities. She hadn't been alone with Max in anything other than a professional setting and she suddenly felt seized with the terror of finding nothing to talk about other than the inn. She supposed they had managed just fine at the diner, but then Lucy always had a way of putting people at ease.

"You're frowning again," Abby pointed out.

Holly shifted her eyes to Abby's reflection and smiled through a sigh. "That better?"

"Nervous?"

Holly felt her shoulders slump in resignation. "Just a little."

Abby's smile widened and Holly could see her eyes begin to dance, even from this distance. "Good, that means you like him."

Of course I like him, Holly thought. "It's just been a while since—"

"Since you've had any fun?"

Holly shrugged and returned to the mirror so she could

add an extra bit of blush to her cheeks. She hadn't really thought about it but, yes, it had been a long time since she'd had any fun...unless you counted knitting circles, book clubs, and Friday movie night with her married guests as fun.

"It's just too bad that he doesn't live closer," Holly said, pursing her lips in displeasure.

"So?" Abby quipped. "A hot guy has asked you out to dinner tonight, Holly. When's the last time that happened?"

Holly pinched her lips and narrowed her gaze at her friend. Abby knew exactly how long it had been and she wasn't about to help prove her point.

"Take it for what it is, Holly! You get to dress up, go out, and have fun. And maybe if you're lucky, the date will last straight through to morning," she added with a mischievous grin.

Holly picked up a cosmetic brush and tossed it in Abby's direction. "Stop it!" She laughed, but she knew Abby wasn't joking.

"What?" Abby cried. "Come on, you can't tell me you haven't thought about it. The man is gorgeous, Holly...you may as well enjoy him!"

Holly shook her head firmly. "I'm not looking for a one-night stand. You know what I'm looking for."

Abby met her sharp gaze and tipped her head in response. "I know...but all I'm saying is...be open-minded. You've been sitting here alone night after night for as many years as you've been running this inn." Abby lay back on the bed and dramatically ran her hands over the cotton comforter. "Has this bed ever experienced anything more exciting than a pair of flannel pajamas and a romance novel?"

Nope, Holly thought, but she couldn't help but laugh.

Abby had a point—Holly *had* closed herself off to love over time. But was Max really the one to make her open to the idea of it again?

Max was already waiting in the lobby when Holly came around the corner at their designated meeting time. He was dressed casually, in dark jeans and a charcoal cashmere sweater. A heavy parka was slung over his arm along with a scarf.

Holly glanced down at her own ensemble, feeling grateful that Abby had stuck around to help her pull together her look. Gone were the uptight work skirt and heels. In her slim-fitting jeans tucked into knee-high leather boots and a black V-neck top, Holly figured she looked equally ready for a night out with a new friend...or something more. As Max's eyes roamed appreciatively over her, she couldn't help but hope it might be the latter.

She smiled shyly. She was attracted to this man like she had never been attracted to any other.

"You got some new clothes!" Holly pointed to the hat in Max's hand.

His face lit up in response to the recognition. "I picked these up in town today."

Understanding took hold. "Ah. So that's when you met Bobby Miller. Interesting kid, that one."

Max shrugged into his heavy coat and zippered it closed. "I warmed up to him by the end," he admitted. "He sort of reminded me a little of myself at that age."

"Really?" Holly hadn't seen that one coming. She couldn't think of anyone who seemed more different than Max than the Miller boy. Max was...well, every adjective Abby had cited earlier that morning. Dashing. Smooth. Warm. Bobby Miller was just...unpleasant.

She couldn't see Max ever behaving that way and she

wasn't sure she wanted to either. Allowing Max to hold the door open for her, she crossed into the cold evening. Snow fell softly on her uncovered head.

"What's this?" Max scolded, lifting a lock of her hair and then letting it drop back against her coat. "You don't have a hat? My, my, Miss Tate. And here I thought I was unprepared."

Holly hadn't wanted to look too casual on her possible date and she now realized her error. "I forgot," she lied with a smile. "It's okay."

Max questioned her with his eyes. "You sure?"

"I'm sure." Holly climbed into the passenger seat of Max's car. She hadn't even considered driving into town. Somehow, without a word, Max had taken charge of the evening.

It felt nice to be the one being taken care of for a change.

"So tell me more about your exchange with Bobby," Holly said, once Max had turned the car off the driveway. She placed her hands in front of the vents to warm them. "I have to admit that I see absolutely no resemblance between the two of you."

Max gave a small smile. "You mean you don't think I have a chip on my shoulder?"

Holly laughed. "No."

"Joking aside," Max said, flicking on the windshield wipers, "I wasn't that much different at one time. I don't know Bobby, of course, but it seemed to me like he wants more from life than Maple Woods can offer."

Holly bridled. "Gee, thanks."

"Oh—Holly, I'm sorry. I didn't mean it like that." Beside her, Max winced.

If he wasn't so damn cute… "It's okay. I know what you meant."

But something inside her twisted. Max had a point about

Bobby. Maple Woods *didn't* offer much. Certainly nowhere near the amount of opportunities that a major city could. If Max saw something of his younger self in Bobby, then it must have meant that a town like Maple Woods wouldn't work for him. That he could understand why Bobby would want to leave. That Maple Woods wasn't glamorous enough.

Already sensing the evening was headed in a disappointing direction, Holly changed the subject, feeling suddenly weary and deflated. "There's a tree lighting in the town square tonight. They always do it the Friday before Christmas."

A long pause followed as Max said nothing. Holly shifted uncomfortably in her leather bucket seat, regretting the suggestion. Max had invited her out, and if city life was something he seemed to so clearly prefer, a tree lighting was probably hardly his idea of an exciting time.

Holly chewed the inside of her lip and battled with the pang in her chest. She had been looking forward to that tree lighting, but she was hardly going to trade it in for a chance to spend the evening with Max.

Finally, Max's warm, thick voice filled the silence. "I have to say, that I'm not sure I've ever met anyone with so much holiday spirit."

The observation was pleasant but Holly detected a subtle, underlying edge. "You make it sound like that's a bad thing."

"Eh."

"You don't celebrate Christmas?"

"Not if I can avoid it," Max said simply and Holly's stomach clenched. It was one thing not to celebrate the holiday, and it was another to actively dislike it. She considered asking Max the reason behind his lack of Christmas spirit, but decided to let it go. The night was already off to a shaky start as it was.

Slumping back into her seat, Holly stared passively out the window at the snow-covered trees, but as soon as Max turned the car onto Main Street, she couldn't help but smile.

The entire street was illuminated by strands of lights wrapped around every lamp post and tree and draped over each shop awning. All along the sidewalk, a festival of lights had been assembled in every color of the rainbow. Santa and his sleigh. A slew of tiny elves. Snowmen, reindeer, and every other Christmas-themed notion. The effect was not short of magical, and cars in front of them slowed to enjoy the display.

"Quite a show," Max said tightly.

"They do it every year," she told him. Her eyes flitted from side to side, eager to take in every lighted object. "It's one of the traditions I love most about this town."

Max had turned to face her, and she distractedly met his stare. Even amidst the sparkle of the light show, she could see the blaze of mirth in his eyes at her reaction.

"I'm sorry," she chuckled, collapsing against her seatback. Her cheeks colored fiercely, and she was grateful he wouldn't notice with all the red lights pouring in from the window. Laughing at herself she said, "Maybe you're right. I really do have more Christmas spirit than most."

Max spared her a lopsided grin. "You're forgiven. Besides, it's kind of cute."

Holly's mouth snapped shut. She had forgotten what she was about to say. She merely stared. Her ability to speak, gone. Max was blissfully unaware of the effect he had on her as he pulled the car to a stop and turned off the ignition.

Cute. He thought she was cute. She replayed the exact words again, just to be sure he had really spoken them.

Butterflies fluttered through Holly's stomach and into her chest. She swallowed hard and stepped out of the car, wishing suddenly that she could climb back inside and have

Max all to herself again. She didn't want to have to share the night with anyone or anything. She wanted to focus all of her attention on him. Without distraction.

Night's like this didn't happen often in her world, and she was determined to commit this evening to memory.

Maybe it would be a story she would one day share with their children.

She banished the thought just as quickly as it formed. Ludicrous! She was getting ahead of herself, and she of all people should know better.

"Why don't we go over to the tree lighting?" Max suggested.

Holly tipped her head. "Oh…it's okay."

"Hey! I'm new in town. You're supposed to be showing me all the local attractions," he teased.

"But I thought you didn't want to go."

He peered at her suspiciously. "I never said that."

Holly flashed back to their conversation. Perhaps he hadn't spoken the exact words, but he had still managed to show a concrete lack of enthusiasm. "Okay, I guess you didn't say that. But seriously, we don't have to go. I've been to this every year. It wouldn't kill me to miss it this one time."

"So it's a tradition for you, is it?" Max began walking toward the center of the square. The decision had been made.

Running the few feet to catch up, Holly asked, "How about you? Any family traditions?"

Max sniffed and shivered in his coat. He avoided eye contact by staring in the shop windows. "Not really."

The answer was less than satisfying. Holly curbed a swell of frustration and tried again. "So, you've already established that you avoid Christmas. What do you usually do instead of celebrating?"

Max shrugged. "Work."

Something inside Holly hardened. Work. She should have known. Why else would he be in town—on business—the week before Christmas?

Holly felt her stomach curdle with disenchantment.

So there it was. A workaholic. She knew the type all too well thanks to Brendan. Men who would rather climb the corporate ladder than be tied down with a wife and kids. Men who only wanted a girlfriend when it was convenient for them. Men who didn't want to be held responsible for anything serious. Men who wanted to work hard and play hard without complications. She should have known, really. Max was gorgeous, unattached, and clearly very successful. It was a common combination. And a lethal one, in her experience.

Her heart contracted with each breath, throbbing with pressure as the reality of the situation became all too clear. It was too good to be true. She should have known. Max was who he was and she was not going to be the girl to try and change him. She'd been a fool once, and she'd be damned if she'd be one again.

He may be cute and rich and have a smile that could make her knees shake, but he'd break her heart without a bat of his curly, black lashes. If she let him.

They began to approach the town square with hands thrust in pockets, chins tucked in scarves, and quietly gathered with the other townspeople who were crowded below the base of a large evergreen. A children's choir was huddled together, waiting for their cue from the elementary school's music teacher.

"Beautiful tree this year, Holly!" someone cried out and Holly beamed.

"That's your tree?" Max whispered, his eyes wide.

"I donate one every year," she said. "With so much land, it's the least I can do."

"The owner doesn't mind?" A frown line creased Max's forehead.

Holly's breath caught. "I'm surprised you would remember that I didn't own the land," she said, feeling slightly uneasy.

But Max just threw her a devastating grin. "I learned a long time ago that when a pretty girl talks, you should listen."

Holly cheeks burned with pleasure and she skirted her eyes to her feet. When she dared to glance his way again, Max was scrutinizing her with an amused smile.

Relief finally came when the children's choir suddenly broke out in song, their small, sweet voices echoing in the night air. A chill descended over the crowd as the mesmerizing, almost haunting sound filled the silence. At the last verse, the tree immediately sprang to life, and the magnificent lights illuminated the crowd's smiling faces.

Max leaned in to her and whispered, "Cold?" The soft touch of his breath so close to her ear as he whispered such a simple question forced a rush of electricity to run the length of Holly's body. She trembled slightly and then quickly drew a sharp gust of freezing air in a vain attempt to regain some form of composure.

Mistaking her shudder for a shiver, Max draped an arm around her shoulder. His dense parka felt like a down blanket as he pulled her in closer. "That better?"

She barely managed a nod. Max's proximity began caving in on her, causing her body to respond in a primal way she had not experienced in a very long time. Even through the thick coat, she could feel the hard wall of his chest as he held her close, and the strong weight of his arm as it enveloped her shoulder, his hand gracing down to rest on her elbow. A flush of desire poured through her blood, heightening her senses. Her mind began to reel with the possibilities of what his body would feel like against hers and she had a swift and all-consuming urge to rip off that parka and press him firmly against her so she could properly feel the contours of his body, and the ripples of his muscled chest.

She knew that indulging herself with these thoughts was pointless. She could never act on them. She would only be disappointed. He was leaving in a matter of days. And he had made it clear where his priorities lay. But it wouldn't hurt to enjoy the moment...

Once the last song had been sung and the last ovation had been given, the group begin to disperse. A crowd was already working its way to Lucy's Place or the pizzeria, not quite ready for the evening to end. Max slipped his arm from her shoulder and said, "I don't know about you, but I'm famished. Shall we?"

He crooked his arm by invitation and wordlessly, Holly slipped her mittened hand through. A surge of longing choked her, drowning her in a sea of desire and conflicting emotion. Her body ached for his touch and the sensation it stirred within her.

She knew she had only just met him. He was, for all intents and purposes, a complete stranger. A stranger here for an extended stay. A workaholic. A bachelor by his own choosing. He was wrong. All wrong.

And Holly knew all at once that she was in very big trouble.

Holly slipped into the chair across from Max and unraveled her scarf from her neck. He watched as she twisted her upper body to hang her coat over the back of her chair, her tiny waist craning, and her breasts pressing against the thin cashmere of her black sweater.

Sitting so close to her, Max felt more alive than ever. The heat of her body so close to his was so intense, the sweet smell of her flowery perfume so feminine, that it took everything in him not to reach down and graze a finger along the small, creamy hand that held her menu.

"So, just so that we're clear, tonight's on me." He watched as Holly lowered her eyes and her features twisted in protest. Before she could speak, he held up a palm. "I insist."

Holly gave a shy smile as she looked up at him from under her long, graceful lashes. "Thank you."

"Now. What's good here?" Max turned the menu over and studied the specials. Lucy's Place was about comfort food, it seemed. Chicken pot pie. Mac and cheese. Fish and chips.

"I'll admit I haven't eaten dinner here very often." Holly's brows knitted as she studied the menu and Max felt himself grow curious.

"Really?" He leaned in closer to study her pretty face. Her soft, full lips were painted with a tinted red gloss that he wanted to kiss right off her mouth. His groin tightened as she met his gaze and he abruptly reached for his water glass to defuse the heat she stirred within him. Desire choked him, closing his throat and making it hard to swallow the icy liquid. He wanted this woman. Badly. But given the circumstances, she was off-limits. His mind knew it, but his body wasn't yet ready to accept it.

"I don't really get out much," she explained. Her hazel eyes darkened at the admission, and he felt a strange affection for her take hold and linger. Holly seemed like a woman surrounded by loving friends. Maybe he had misunderstood.

"Life at the inn keeps me so busy," she continued. "We serve dinner every night, so it usually makes sense for me to just eat there."

Max held her gaze with his, searching for something in

them beyond her explanation. He couldn't be certain, but he thought he detected a shadow creeping over her face.

"Well, they have wine," he noted, pulling his eyes from hers to glance back at the menu. "Want to share a bottle?"

Holly brightened. "Sure."

"White or red?"

"Red for the winter. White for summer."

Max's lips twitched. She was a funny little thing. "Red it is then."

The waitress he remembered from earlier came over to their table, grinning at Holly. "Isn't this a pleasant surprise," she said.

"Hey, Emily," Holly said. She glanced at Max, pinching her pretty little lips. "I was just telling Max that I don't get out much for dinner."

"Not enough," Emily said. "Guess it takes someone special to drag her away from the job."

From the corner of his vision, Max could see a flush appear on Holly's cheeks. He couldn't deny the twist of pleasure that stirred his belly.

"I'm Max," he said abruptly to the waitress, forcing away thoughts that shouldn't linger. "I saw you this morning, but didn't catch your name."

The young woman smiled warmly. "Emily Porter," she said. "So what can I get you?"

Max placed the order and turned his attention back to Holly, his anxiety growing in their small silences. He needed to keep pressing forward, keep talking to her. If he stopped and thought about what he was doing, he'd stand up and leave. He knew better than to be sitting here with her right now, but he was powerless to his own desire. He liked this woman, and it had been a long time since he had felt this way about anyone. Normally, the first sense of heartfelt interest made him start thinking of an excuse to end things quickly, but not so with Holly. It went beyond the way his gut tightened in response to her natural feminine curves. It was something in her voice. In her smile. Something that touched him on a level he was unfamiliar with. Something that made his heart ache.

Of all people.

"I was sorry to see Evelyn leave," he confided. "I was starting to like having her around."

Holly smiled and tucked her menu behind the napkin holder. "I was afraid she would scare you off."

"It takes a lot to scare me off."

Holly dropped her eyes once more and her lashes fluttered against her rosy cheeks. He hadn't noticed how shy she could be, and her sudden vulnerability made the man in him want to wrap his arms around her and take care of her forever.

He gritted his teeth. How ironic that the one person she needed protecting from was himself.

"Is she always like that?" he asked, pushing down the guilt as best he could. He buried it deep in the pit of his stomach and focused on their conversation.

Holly arched a brow. "Meddlesome, you mean?"

Max chuckled, recalling Evelyn sitting in his room earlier that afternoon regaling him with tales of other guests she'd had the pleasure—or displeasure moreover—of meeting over her many semiannual visits. "Yeah, I don't even know the best word to describe her. She's certainly one of a kind."

Holly slipped him a secret smile. "I think she had a crush on you."

Max felt himself blush and he broke out in laughter to cover his embarrassment. "She seems like a very special lady."

"She is." Holly cast him a challenging look, as if gauging his tolerance. "I remember one time she thought another guest was hitting on Nelson."

A peal of laughter sputtered out of Max's lips. *"What?"*

"I know." Holly rolled her eyes at the memory but the twisting of her lips betrayed her fondness for it. "It seems silly, but she was just convinced this woman was flirting with Nelson. I mean, convinced. She couldn't let it go. She went after that poor woman in the blueberry patch for asking Nelson to help her find a new bucket. Chased her all the way back to the barn."

"What about Nelson?"

Holly waved a hand through the air dismissively. "He just stood there and watched. Completely bewildered."

Max shook his head, wishing he could have been there. "She's a firecracker."

Holly tipped her head to the side. Her eyes roamed over his face lazily. "That's a *very* good description."

"Well, thank you," Max said, grinning.

Emily brought the wine to the table and he sipped at his glass, enjoying the anecdotes about the inn. The more Holly talked, the more captivated he became. She was a compelling woman with a knack for putting people at ease. No wonder she was so at home at the inn; why she made so many others feel at home there, too. She was sweet in a quiet, nurturing sort of way. Her world seemed calm. Peaceful. For a moment, he dared himself to imagine what it would be like to live in that world.

He had an uneasy feeling that he would like it there.

He knew he could ask her, right then and there, when she was reminiscing about experiences at the inn, if she would ever think of giving it up, moving back to the city. But for some reason, he couldn't. Now wasn't the time. If she said no, he would be left with no alternative but to admit the truth. This dinner—and any hope of others to come—would grind to a halt. Any chance of getting to know her better would be gone. She was a trusting sort, and he couldn't take complete advantage of her. So for now, he'd rather not know her stance.

Besides, there was always a chance that he'd sway her view, especially if she was as charmed with him as he was by her.

After all, he still had five days until Christmas.

The diner looked different this evening than it had earlier in the day. The lights were dimmed and the room was lit predominantly by dozens of strands of multicolored lights. Around the perimeter of the walls, an electronic train worked its way around the room. Max smiled as he watched it go around, the sight of it filling his chest with an ache he couldn't fight.

"I remember asking Santa for a train like that one year," he said.

At the mention of Christmas, presumably, Holly perked up. "Did you get it?"

"No."

Holly's forehead creased into a frown. She clearly hadn't been expecting that response. "Oh. That's sad."

Max shrugged and watched silently as the train passed by them once more. "North Pole Express," he mused, reading the label. "That's a good one."

Holly watched it passively, her attention fixed on his story. "Did you get the train the next year?" she asked hopefully.

"Oh, it was too late by then," Max said evenly. He inhaled deeply, wishing he had never mentioned the train. Or Christmas.

"Why's that?"

"Because by then, I no longer believed in Santa." He

managed a smile and quickly shifted the conversation. "I hope it's okay that I'm sticking around through Christmas."

Holly drifted her eyes from the train to his. "I'm really happy you're staying, actually."

His stomach tightened. He didn't know whether to feel guilty or excited or both. "I'm not intruding on any plans?"

Holly tucked a strand of chestnut hair behind her ear and toyed with the stem of her wine glass. She cast her eyes downward. "I tend to rely on my guests for company." She dragged her attention away from her glass and watched him with a guarded edge. "You really spend your Christmas working most years?"

"Don't you?"

Holly stiffened, but the corner of her lip curled into a smile. "Touché."

Max drew a sharp breath. "I don't mind working. And Christmas is…highly overrated."

She watched him with a critical squint, her eyes darkening. After a pause she gave a noncommittal "Maybe."

Max suspected she didn't hold the same view. Her outward joy at anything related to the holiday was proof. She couldn't cover up her feelings even if she tried. And he was glad she wasn't trying. He liked a woman who could hold her own. Holly was true to herself.

And true to those around her. A ripple of shame passed through him.

"Do you celebrate at all? Even just to get together for a party with friends?" She watched him carefully, searching his face for an explanation.

"It's not my thing."

Holly's eyes narrowed slightly, but her attention was quickly pulled to a man approaching the table.

"George!" she said, smiling once more.

"Nice to see you in here this time of evening, Holly. I hope I'm not, uh, interrupting you."

Holly's cheeks turned a fleeting shade of pink. "I don't think you've been introduced," she said. "This is Max Hamilton, a guest at the inn. Max, this is George Miller. He and Lucy own the diner."

Max stiffened. He held out a hand. "Pleased to meet you," he said, giving George a firm handshake. "I met your wife and son this morning."

"Max is already a fan of Lucy's pies," Holly chimed in.

"My second time here today," Max said. "And I only just arrived last night."

George grinned. "Already a regular, then!"

Max managed a thin smile, feeling sly and underhanded. This wasn't like him, but he didn't know what else to do. "Guess so."

"How long are you in town?" George continued. Across from Max, Holly stared at him expectantly.

"Through the holiday," he replied.

"Family here?"

"Just me."

George's eyes narrowed in surprise but he recovered quickly. Refilling Holly's wine glass, he said, "Let us know if you need anything. We like to keep our customers happy."

Max gave a watery smile. "Just like Holly."

"Must be something in the air." George inched back as the door jingled and a new pair of customers shuffled in from the cold. He lifted his chin and raised a hand in greeting. "Better go seat them. But good to meet you, Max. Hopefully I'll be seeing you again before you head out."

"I'm sure of it," Max said.

More sure than you know. He turned to Holly. "Shall we?" he asked, tipping his head toward the door. "I wouldn't mind walking around town before the storm hits."

She nodded. "Another glass of this wine and you'd be carrying me back to the inn."

"Would that be so bad?" Max asked, and Holly's cheeks flared.

"If I didn't know better, I might think you were trying to flirt with me," she said as she shrugged into her coat and buttoned it closed.

Max watched her thoughtfully, noticing the way her eyes blazed a brighter shade, the way the high color in her cheeks set off the tint of ruby in her lips.

"Maybe I am," he murmured.

Holly pressed her lips together, but he could tell she was pleased. Maybe none of this was as complicated as he worried it would be. Holly was young, single and trapped in Maple Woods. Sure, she loved her inn, but that didn't mean she wouldn't embrace change. She had lived in Boston before this, after all.

"Do you ever get back to Boston?" he asked, holding the door for her.

Holly wound her scarf tighter around her neck and began leading them down the snow-covered sidewalk. "Not really," she said, stopping to glance at a window display in the stationery store. "The inn keeps me so busy, I can't exactly get away without closing down business."

"That must be difficult," Max ventured.

Holly sighed, releasing a plume of steam into the brittle night air. "Oh, life is full of sacrifices, I suppose."

Max frowned at her choice of words, wondering if he should dare to read more meaning into them than she'd intended. She loved the inn, that much was clear in the way she lit up around her guests or when she spoke of the place, but she'd chosen to give something up to keep it going. Max knew well enough what happened when people sacrificed too much for one thing. Eventually they came to resent it, and soon after, they left it. Just as his mother had.

Falling into easy silence, they walked a lap around the town square, their feet crunching over the frozen snow, pausing here and there so Holly could enjoy the decorations, until the wind picked up and the snowflakes grew thick and wet.

"We should probably head back to the inn," Holly said, looking up to the sky.

Disappointment settled heavy in his chest as they approached the car. As the lights from the town faded behind them and The White Barn Inn came into view, Max had a momentary vision of the bulldozers coming and knocking it to the ground, leveling it to a field and later paving it with cement. Only a matter of weeks ago, he had gazed at the plot of land and imagined his sleek shopping center standing proudly at the edge, but now the thought of this big, beautiful house being gone felt sad and unfair.

He turned to Holly as he pulled the car to a stop and popped his seat belt. Letting go of the past was hard—he'd learned that at an early age. But letting go of the past was the only thing that kept you moving forward. Surely, Holly would be the better for it? Maybe this was the opportunity she needed to start living for herself instead of always taking care of others.

"I had a lot of fun tonight," Holly said as they slipped through the front door. Just off the foyer, the lobby area was dimly lit and the fireplace was dark. Not a sound could be heard through the giant house, forcing all of Max's attention on the beautiful girl in front of him.

"See, it's fun to get out and go to dinner once in a while."

She gave a slow smile as she looked up at him. "You're right," she admitted. "I think I do need to get out a bit more."

He hesitated, lured in by the slight parting of her lips, the lingering hold in her gaze, by the awareness that there was no one else in this house but the two of them.

"I should go check some emails," he said, his voice husky and low. Firm. He was convincing himself, not her, and he was doing a damn poor job of it.

Her cheerful expression faded ever so softly, and without thinking, knowing only that he didn't want to see that look cross her face or know that he had caused it, he reached out and set a hand on her arm and leaned down. She blinked up at him, her eyes flashing in awareness of their sudden proximity, and then he turned his head ever so slightly and brushed her cheek with his mouth. Her skin was smooth and light against his lips, and his groin tightened at her sweet smell. Everything in him was telling him to graze his mouth to hers, to taste her lips.

Max stepped back. Not tonight. Not with the conversation with George Miller on the table.

He was still in town for four more days. And in that time period, anything was possible.

Chapter Six

"Good morning," Max said from the kitchen entrance, his voice deliciously thick and scratchy from slumber. Holly's heart lurched and she felt the color drain from her face as she turned to sweep her eyes over his chiseled, unshaven face. Her pulse quickened as his mouth tipped into a knowing grin, and his blue eyes twinkled. She knew he would most likely come into the kitchen—it was breakfast time after all—but the sudden sight of him standing there was still enough to send a shock through her and she found herself completely flustered and unprepared.

Max leaned against the doorjamb, tall and strong, folding two thick arms across his broad chest. His hair, she noticed, was slick and wet, and a vivid image of him in a shower with water streaming down his hard body flashed through her mind before she could stop herself. Instinctively, she brought her hand to her mouth and bit down on the side of her thumb, staring at the object of her desire under the hood of her long lashes.

It had been a long, sleepless night.

"Hey!" she replied, gathering her wits. She had to pull it together today; she'd promised herself that much. She was going to behave today. She had to.

He was all wrong for her. A workaholic who didn't even live in town. And—though she was quick to forget— he was her guest.

Amazing how quickly both facts could mean so little when he strolled into her kitchen looking like that.

Max ventured farther into the sun-filled warmth of the kitchen. He crossed behind her to the coffeepot on the counter and his hip brushed casually against hers. Something flipped inside her at the involuntary connection.

This was going to be more difficult than she thought.

She pressed her lips together, fighting her weakening resolve. She had tossed and turned all night thinking of the way Max's sharp blue eyes had pierced hers last night, the way his lips had tenderly brushed her cheek when he said goodnight. The way his strong, heavy hand had lingered on her arm. The way her heart had missed him from the second he turned and ascended the stairs to his room. The way her bed had never felt so vast. Or so empty.

She still didn't know if their evening had constituted a real date, but it was real all right. Too real. So real that she feared it would take her a long time to forget it and come back to reality. Because the reality was that in four days Max would be gone and she would be all alone.

And the reality she knew before his arrival had somehow come unraveled in the two days since she'd first set eyes on him.

How strange that only a couple of days ago she was so content with her life, so seemingly fulfilled, and now all she could think about was how much she was missing. She'd always known how much she wanted a family of her own, but she'd managed to fill that hole in her heart—and this house—with a makeshift family. The variety of personalities shuffling in and out of The White Barn Inn made this old mansion a home. But Max's arrival served the opposite purpose of the coming of her other guests. Instead of warming her heart, it just made it ache.

She liked him more than she wanted to. And the harder part was that she thought he might like her, too.

She chewed her lip in thought. New York *was* only two hours away...

No. She banished the notion immediately. Maple Woods was her home. It had given her a sense of community that she had never known. A feeling of belonging. Of comfort. Of safety and security. She had a place here. A purpose. She could never leave it all behind.

Recalling his words last night, it was to Holly's chagrin that she knew Max preferred a much different way of life. It was just one of the many strikes she held against him.

But then...what were the others? Her mind was clouded by his all-consuming presence; she was so rattled she couldn't even remember if she'd salted the eggs yet. Or if she'd set the timer for the toast. She was a mess, and the more desperate she became to find composure, the more fuzzy her thoughts grew.

With a mental flip of a coin, she grabbed the saltshaker and doused the eggs. It was a gamble, but it would have to do. Besides, keeping her hands busy with her task was the only way to keep them from innocently wandering over to Max and doing things they really shouldn't.

Max leaned against the counter and took a gulp from his mug. "I have to ask. What exactly do you put in this coffee? Or...is it a secret?"

"Cinnamon."

"Ah," Max said, taking another sip. His lips turned into an easy smile. "Nice touch."

"Thanks," she said. She sprinkled some rosemary over the diced potatoes that were sizzling in the frying pan, grateful for an excuse to look away from that irresistible face. Her knees felt weak just sensing his rugged body so close to hers.

For not the first time since he'd entered the room, she wished he'd just grab her and press her close to that hard, ripped chest.

You stop it, she chastised herself. Honestly, this was getting out of control. She was powerless to her own desire for him. It wasn't like her.

Leave it to Max to unleash a whole side of her she didn't even know existed.

"Looks like the snow has stopped," Max observed.

Holly looked up from the stove and followed his gaze out the window over the sink. Only a mere two feet of snow had gathered over night—hardly the snowstorm of the year that the forecast had warned. Not that she was complaining. The threat of more had left her alone with Max; she couldn't have orchestrated the outcome better if she had tried. She almost had to laugh over the irony of her concern only twenty-four hours ago, when the thought of everyone checking out early had seemed so devastating. Amazing how sometimes things just worked out the way they were meant to. If she were more of a romantic sort, she might have called it fate. "Maple Woods is used to handling snow like this. I'm sure the roads will be plowed in two hours."

"Look like a lot to me," Max said, eyes fixed out the window. "But I guess the road conditions are the biggest factor."

"Does that mean you'll be leaving early?" Her heart

flipped as she spoke. She didn't know what was keeping him in town. The weather. Business. Or her.

"That eager to get rid of me?" His eyes danced at the banter.

She took his response as a no, her chest rising and falling with relief. "I hope you like omelets."

"You don't need to cook."

"Of course I do. You're still my guest."

"Holly." His tone was deep in sound, gentle in protest. He dropped his head to the side, his eyes locking with hers. A heavy silence took over the room.

Holly drew a shaky breath. "I told Stephen to take the rest of the week off, so hopefully my cooking will do."

"If it's anything like yesterday morning, I'll be a happy man."

"Good. Why don't you pick a spot and I'll bring everything in," she said, feeling nervous under his watchful eye.

"You're not going to make me eat alone, are you?" He lifted an eyebrow and pulled himself from the counter.

"Of course not. I'll be out in ten minutes." She kept her eyes on the frying pan until he finally left the kitchen and only then did she release an enormous pent-up breath. She clutched the counter and bent over it, feeling all at once dizzy and lightheaded. She stood to fan her face as her body temperature continued to rise.

The effect that man had over her was unparalleled. And ridiculous. She filled a glass with cold water from the tap and took a long sip, tipping her head back to consume every last drop, and set it back on the counter. After wiping the back of her hand over her mouth, she fanned her face once more, taking deep breaths to calm her pounding heart.

Honestly. Was this what she had come to, spending year after year holed up in this house? By the way she was responding to his slightest flirtation, you would have thought she'd been living in a convent!

She grinned wryly to herself. Considering she hadn't dated anyone since leaving Boston, the analogy had more truth in it than she cared to admit.

Gathering her wits once more, Holly finished preparing breakfast and carried the food into the dining room. Surprised to find it empty, she set the heavy tray down on the nearest table and ducked her head into the lobby. Max was sitting on a leather club chair, an ankle propped on the opposite knee, a cell phone clutched to his ear. He promptly ended the call when he spotted her.

"You didn't need to hang up on account of me," she said as she neared him. "I would have waited."

Max waved away her concerns. "Nah. Just business. Boring stuff."

There was that word again. Business.

"Well, breakfast is ready when you are."

Max rose to his feet and Holly reflexively raked her eyes over the length of his body. "Smells good," he said.

"Thanks," she said, crossing back into the dining room. She arranged the plates on the table and pulled out a chair to join him. "Do you have any plans for the day?"

As soon as she said the words, she immediately regretted them, fearing her phrasing might be misconstrued as an invitation. Not that she wouldn't mind spending the day with Max, but she didn't want to seem…needy.

"I have some work to do this morning in town," he said and Holly felt a twinge of dismay.

"I'll be in town today, too, actually," she said, remembering her own plans with relief. "Every weekend in December the town hosts a Christmas Market in the town square. I help out each year."

"See?" He waved a fork playfully in her direction. "You work through the holidays, too. It's not just me."

"It's different." Holly bristled. "I'm still participating in the holiday."

Max met her stare from the corner of his eye. He didn't buy it.

"Don't you ever feel like you're missing out on Christmas?" she asked.

Max cut into his omelet. "Christmas doesn't hold any meaning to me. No good feelings, at least."

Holly frowned, and something deep inside her seared open. She swallowed hard, pushing away the thought before it could surface. "I'm sorry to hear that."

Max shrugged and reached for his coffee mug. "No sympathy needed. I have work to keep me busy through the holiday. It's not like I feel I'm missing anything." He smiled tightly, holding her eyes for a fleeting second, before lowering his gaze to his plate.

"Hmm," Holly said, watching him carefully. His jaw seemed hardened as he focused on his food.

"Besides," Max continued, "Christmas is for children, for families. I have neither."

That makes two of us, she thought grimly. "Do you ever wish you could leave the office behind for a few days, maybe…make time for a child or family?" she ventured.

Max chewed a wedge of toast thoughtfully. "I try not to wish for things that can't happen."

Can't or won't?

She supposed it didn't matter. The heaviness in Holly's heart was replaced with emptiness at his words. His work was his life. By his choosing. And it didn't seem as though he was open to sacrificing his time. Or making an effort. It didn't seem as if anything more held any meaning to him.

Sadness coated her stomach. He was confirming her

worst suspicions. He wanted to focus on a career, not everything else that mattered so much to her.

An old wound opened. She'd still never forgotten the way she felt returning home after that last dinner with Brendan. Thinking it was the night he was going to propose, she'd bought a dress just for the occasion and even splurged on a manicure at a little spa around the corner from her apartment. All through dinner she could barely eat, so sick was she with anticipation, wondering how he would do it, what the ring would look like, what she would say. Would he get down on one knee?

But Brendan had no intention of proposing that night. Or any night. The romantic occasion had been his way of telling her that he was being transferred to Los Angeles. He had no intention of returning to Boston and at no point in the conversation did he broach the idea of her moving with him, not that she would have wanted to go. Her grandmother was all she had by then, and her parents' sudden death six months prior was still unbearably fresh. Staying in close proximity to Maple Woods and her grandmother was too important.

Watching Brendan's beaming face nearly burst with pride over his promotion, without any regard for the heartache she was feeling at his expense, without any consideration for the two years of her life she had given him, she couldn't help wonder what she had done wrong. Knowing that there was nothing she could have said or done to make him want to stay, she had reached the obvious conclusion. The only thing she was at fault for was giving her heart to the wrong man. When she looked back and thought of the time she had spent with him, spending so many weekends in Boston when she could have spent more time in Maple Woods with the last of her family, she felt a pang of regret so deep, she thought it would break her.

And that was a mistake she was determined to never repeat again.

With a hardened heart she went on a few dates over the years, but the pickings were slim in Maple Woods and eventually she just stopped altogether. But still, she dared to hope that someday she'd find a family of her own again. That her home would be filled with love and laughter and memories.

As an only child of two deceased parents, all she wanted was someone to share her life with. It was a simple thing to wish for, wasn't it?

George Miller lived in a small house behind the diner. He'd agreed to meet Max there, rather than in the open setting of Lucy's Place, where they would be sure to garner suspicion from the other locals. Max had been brief in their phone conversation, not even stating the nature of the visit and only hinting that he was a real estate developer when he asked George if they might talk at his convenience. If George was curious about the reason for the meeting, he didn't reveal it.

George was shoveling the front sidewalk when Max rolled to a stop. "Come on in," he said, propping the shovel against the front porch. "Lucy's at the diner and Bobby's out with friends, so the house is quiet. I'm afraid I don't have much time. I need to get back to the diner in about half an hour."

Max pounded the snow off his boots on the mat and followed George into the cramped living room. "Is Bobby still in school?" he asked.

"Winter break," George replied.

"Ah," Max said.

"Those were the days, weren't they?" George said ruefully, and Max felt his lips thin.

He had loved the academic side of school—the distraction and hope that reading and learning provided. When he was very young, he looked forward to the school year, seeing it as an escape from his unhappy home life. By the time he was in middle school, his classmates had grown mean, and Max dreaded the shame he felt from the judgment in the eyes of his classmates, the pity in the faces of his teachers. They knew all about his father—about the brawls down at the bar, about the black eyes and drunken tirades. Those who lived close enough heard the doors slamming, the glass breaking as it hit the walls. They saw the flashing lights from the police cruisers late at night. It was a common sight, but the dread Max felt the next day never faded.

And they all knew about his mother, of course…. His teachers had been particularly kind to him as a result, he knew. But he didn't want their sympathy. He didn't want anyone's sympathy.

Holly's words that morning at breakfast had made him pause. He'd almost opened up to her then and there. What had he been thinking? He didn't open up to anyone. Those who knew his story taunted and teased or felt sorry for him. He didn't want anyone to think that way of him again.

"I loved school, actually," Max managed. And despite it all, he had. He'd considered dropping out more than once by the time he was in high school, but he knew that a good education was his only chance at a better life, so he stuck with it. *And look at me now,* he thought. He should feel proud, he should feel successful, but being here in the Miller house, a house not much bigger than the one he'd grown up in, just depressed the hell out of him.

It was this damn town, he told himself. It was making him soft. Making him wish for things he could never have.

"Is Bobby a senior?" Max inquired, shifting his thoughts back to the conversation.

"A junior," George replied.

"I imagine he's busy applying to colleges, then. Isn't this the year for it?"

George dodged the question by taking Max's coat and hanging it in a hall closet. Eventually he said, "We'll see about college. He's hoping for a scholarship. He's quite good at football."

Max nodded, thinking of how quickly circumstances could change.

"So you're staying at The White Barn Inn?" George asked, sinking down into a well-worn armchair.

Max took a seat on a sofa, noticing the threadbare quality of the fabric. "I am," he said. "It's a beautiful establishment."

"Holly does a good job with it," George mused. "She's a sweetheart, that one."

Max allowed himself an internal grimace. It seemed Holly had succeeded in charming the whole town, not just him. "I take it you know her well?"

"She's friendly with my wife. Lucy supplies the inn with those pies you like so much."

Max gave an easy smile. "Your wife is very talented."

George did a poor job at masking his pride. "What can I say? I'm a lucky man."

Looking around the cramped, simple room, Max had a moment of clarity. George *was* happy with his life. It didn't suit Max's needs any more than it seemed to suit Miller's son, but to George it was enough.

And that wasn't good. Max had thought it impossible for the Millers to turn down the sum he was ready to offer, but now he wasn't so sure. They didn't seem to yearn for much more than they had. They were uncomfortably friendly with Holly. What reason would they have to sell the land to him?

If it wasn't for cold hard cash, than what other motivation could he give them?

"Has Lucy thought about branching out with her pies?" Max asked.

"Oh, she's got dreams of opening a little bakery," George said, "but she's too busy running the diner to pursue that right now. He smiled fondly. "She wants to call it Sweetie Pie. She's been saving for years, but it hasn't added up to much."

"You could bring in extra help at the diner to free up her time for another business," Max offered.

"Help doesn't come free, and neither does another rent payment," George replied and Max felt a flicker of hope spark. "We'd hoped Bobby would help out more at the diner, but he's too busy running around with his friends to roll up his sleeves on our account."

Max rearranged himself on the couch and gave a benign smile. It wasn't his place to comment on a situation he had only just come into.

"Lucy thinks getting him out of Maple Woods for a while will be good for him, but I'm not so sure. The kid needs to grow up and once he does, I think he'll decide to follow in his old man's footsteps. We'd love for him to take over the diner one day, maybe grow it into something bigger even."

Max said nothing, using the time instead to consider his best approach. George Miller was a man of deep roots. He was tied to Maple Woods. The situation—from Max's view—was bleak.

"Enough about me," George finally said. "You wanted to meet with me and I have to say, I'm curious. What can I help you with?"

Max inhaled deeply. This was it. If George Miller shot him down, his efforts in Maple Woods would be finished.

His purpose for staying gone. He'd have to head back to New York immediately to start salvaging the project and he would most likely never see Holly again. If George turned him down, news of Max's attempts to swipe her home out from under her would travel back shortly, possibly before he'd even have time to pack his bags and peel out of town.

"My company, Hamilton Properties, is a major retail developer. We have centers throughout the country. Twenty-six in total."

George nodded his head gravely. "Impressive."

"I'll get right to the point, George. For some time now my company has been strategizing to build a shopping center approximately halfway between Boston and New York City. We've done extensive research and planning, including securing several major retailers in order to get the bank to approve the loan. All of these efforts are hinging on one thing, location. We've pulled the demographics and we've driven around several sites. We feel very strongly that your parcel would be the ideal location for our center."

George's jaw slacked. "My parcel? You mean…The White Barn Inn?"

Max was brisk. "Yes."

Gobsmacked, George sat back in his chair, saying nothing as he digested the information. "Wow. I don't even know what to say."

"I understand this must feel random. I wasn't informed that you owned the land until two days ago."

"Are you aware that I have a verbal agreement with Holly Tate to sell her that land?"

Max swallowed the bitter taste in his mouth. "Yes, I'm aware. Is this why you never put the land up for sale before? A parcel of this size is worth a lot of money."

George's brow creased with trouble. "Holly's our friend.

Her family has leased the land for generations... It just didn't feel like it was ours to sell."

"Well, I can assure you it is your land to sell."

George's expression fell and after a beat, he tossed up his hands. "I've had this arrangement in place with her for... years. I'm supposed to transfer the deed to her on Christmas Day. It's already been decided. I'm...I'm sorry, but I'm afraid you're too late."

Max blew out a breath. Slipping his hand into the leather briefcase at his feet, he pulled out the offer he had drawn up before coming to Maple Woods. He extended his arm across the coffee table to George. "If you wouldn't mind taking a look at this before you make your decision, I'd appreciate it. I'm under the impression that there is nothing legally binding the sale to Holly at this point, correct?"

"That's correct. However, there was a stipulation in the original lease that said the lessee—Holly's family—would have first rights to the purchase of the property on the expiration of their lease. That thing is ninety-nine years old. And here we are, less than a week before it expires." George sighed and reached for the paper Max was extending. The color drained from his face as his eyes scanned the page.

"It's a fair price for the land, I can assure you," Max said evenly. He could only imagine what George Miller must be thinking right now. Though he didn't know how much Holly and the Millers had agreed on for the purchase of the land, he thought it safe to assume it was less than five percent of the offer he was making.

"What about Holly?" George asked when he managed to find his voice.

"So long as we come to an agreement before Christmas Day when the lease expires, I don't think there should be a problem." Max cleared his throat. He had four days before that land essentially transferred to Holly for a fraction of its value, and he couldn't risk trying to sway her to sell. His best bet was dealing directly with George Miller.

"And the inn?"

Max's stomach tightened.

"I'm afraid it will have to be razed." He paused. *May as well say it.* "The barns would have to be torn down, as well. I understand there are some orchards. Those would be leveled. Basically, everything would have to be cleared to leave room for the foundation and the parking lot. A center of this size requires a lot of land."

"But why our land, specifically? Surely there must be other—"

Max shook his head. "No. Believe me. A lot of time has gone into finding the perfect location for this development. We have to look at the size of the parcel, the proximity to competing centers, the distance to major highways, the general age range and income of the population within radiuses of various mileages. Consumer behavior... I could continue, if you'd like."

"And all that led you to our land?"

"Yes." Max steepled his fingers and looked down at the scuffed floorboards. swallowed hard and gritted his teeth. Everything he was stating was a fact. A cold, hard fact. There was no other option. The only way for this development to flourish was if it was built on the land that housed Holly's inn.

So why was he having so much trouble accepting that himself?

George let out a long whistle and looked around the crowded room, processing some inner thought. "Understand the position I'm in, Max. Holly is a dear friend of my wife's and I'm fond of her as well. The town loves her. And that inn—everyone loves that inn."

"I wish I could say we could save the inn, but we can't.

It sits too far back from the road, and it cuts into too much of the acreage. Believe me when I say that I wish it could be different. But…it can't." Now that his plans were being spoken aloud and set into motion, Max felt dizzy with guilt. The metallic taste in his mouth was a physical reminder of how corrupt his behavior was, even to himself. He meant what he said, that he wished this could be different. But he was a realist, and he knew that some things just were what they were. And he was going to tear down The White Barn Inn the first chance he had.

"Will the town even approve this?" George asked.

"That's a good question," Max said. "I spoke to the mayor yesterday. He said it was your decision. If you agreed to the sale, the plans for the mall would go to a vote with the planning committee."

"Does anyone else know?"

"No, and I think it's best if we keep it that way," Max said as his thoughts again drifted to Holly. "The mayor would rather not make this public knowledge as he antici- pates a polarizing reaction from the community. If you de- cide to sell the land to me, I'll call him and let him know and he will take it from there."

George opened his eyes wide as the enormity of the de- cision he was faced with became a reality.

"If the planning committee doesn't approve the mall, I have a clause in the contract that permits Hamilton Prop- erties to rescind the offer," Max explained.

George lowered his eyes to read over the papers once more. "I'd like to take some time to talk this over with Lucy."

"Of course," Max said. "But please bear in mind that time is running out. If you agree to sell to me, I will need some time to put the project before the planning commit- tee, and Christmas is only four days away."

"I'll have an answer to you one way or the other as soon as I can," George assured him. He rose from the armchair and Max held out a hand.

"Thank you for your time," Max said. "And if we can keep this from Holly, I'd appreciate it. I know Lucy and she are friends, but I'd rather not have to upset her if there isn't reason to."

"I couldn't agree more," George said. He handed Max his parka and shoved his hands into his jeans. "You're sure there would be no way to save the inn? Put the mall behind it maybe?"

Max shook his head. "Impossible. The blueprints are all drawn up and there simply isn't room. The inn is located in the middle of the planned parking structure. There's no other way to allow for enough spaces. I can show you the drawings if you'd like. They're in my car."

George waved his hand dismissively. "No, no. I just thought I'd ask. If you say it won't work then I trust you."

Trust me. Max clenched a fist, feeling suddenly suffocated and claustrophobic. The parka was too heavy to wear inside. The ceilings were too low. The room too stuffy. He needed air. He needed to breathe and clear his head and stop, stop, stop thinking about Holly.

Holly trusted him, too. And look what he was doing to her right under her nose. He wished he could just tell her, admit the truth, convince her to leave Maple Woods and start building a life for herself, but he didn't think he could. Yet.

"I'll be in touch," George said as Max trotted down the porch stairs to the driveway, gasping for the cold fresh air.

Max climbed into his rental car and turned the ignition, desperate to get out of George's driveway before anyone spotted his New York plates. He realized as he gripped the steering wheel that he was shaking. The magnitude of what he had just done was taking effect. He felt confused, lost and out of control. He hadn't felt this way in years—he had made it a point to avoid ever having to feel this way again. He lived his life in a self-preserving way. And then...then he had met Holly.

The offer was made. It was in George Miller's hands now. And only one thing was certain. There was no going back now.

Chapter Seven

By midmorning, the Christmas Market was vibrant and crowded as familiar faces strolled through the town square clutching steaming paper cups of hot chocolate and snacking on roasted chestnuts. It seemed the entire town had made it out that morning, despite the couple feet of snow that had gathered overnight. Holly had snagged the cart just next to Lucy, who had been up all night making fresh pies in preparation for the festivities. The Saturday before Christmas was always the busiest, and Holly expected to sell what was left of her homemade preserves before the market closed for the day, as she did every year. No matter how much time she spent preserving and jarring the blueberries she had harvested, it seemed there was never enough to keep up with the demand. She'd worked long into the night for weeks in preparation for the annual tradition, but she didn't mind. Keeping busy, she had learned, was a good way to keep from giving in to the loneliness that sometimes crept in late at night, when the guests had turned in and the house grew quiet.

"Where's George?" Holly asked, as she pulled some more jars from a box at her feet.

"He had some bookkeeping to do at the house this morning," Lucy said. "But I doubt he'll make it to the market today. Someone has to cover the diner. We can't leave the staff unsupervised all day."

"Guess not." Holly shivered and turned on her heat lamp. "At least the sun's out today."

"Some big storm," Lucy said ruefully. "Did all your guests head out early just in case it hit hard?"

Holly hesitated. "All but one."

Lucy slid her a glance from her neighboring stall. "Don't tell me. That man who came into the diner yesterday. The one who likes my pies."

Holly's face flushed with heat despite the frost in the air. "None other."

Lucy let out a long whistle. "Well, looks like Christmas came early for you this year!"

Holly lowered her eyes but she couldn't resist a smile. "It's not like that."

"No?" Lucy didn't look convinced. "Because it sure looked like something to me. Do you like him?"

What's not to like? Holly wanted to say. But something in her sinking heart told her there was plenty not to like. She paused to consider the question, knowing it required no thought at all. She did like him. Of course she did. But Max was sadly all wrong for her.

"He lives in New York," Holly explained.

"So?"

"So, that's two hours away." Holly gave her friend a measured stare but Lucy looked unimpressed with her excuse.

"People move all the time," Lucy said casually. She

pulled an apple crumble pie from a box and placed it on a cake platter.

"I think he prefers city life," Holly continued.

"You grew up in Boston," Lucy pointed out. "Would you ever consider going back to that kind of life?"

Holly grimaced. She didn't even want to think about leaving Maple Woods and she felt agitated by how ahead of herself she was getting. "He doesn't seem to want the same things I do."

Lucy pulled a face. "That's too bad. He seemed really interested in you to me."

Holly's heart spasmed. "Really?" Her mind raced as she flashed through the sequence of their conversation at the diner yesterday morning. She was itching to ask Lucy for more specifics on her observation.

Taking notice of Holly's inner struggle, Lucy's lips twisted in satisfaction. "Aha! I *knew* you liked him."

"Of course she likes him!" Abby sauntered up to Holly's cart and handed her a cup of cocoa. Eyes gleaming, she asked, "So how was last night?"

"What was last night?" Lucy inquired, perking up in interest.

"Our little Holly had a date," Abby announced proudly.

"What?" Lucy squealed. "And you didn't blurt it out as soon as you saw me? Holly, we have been here for over an hour. When were you going to mention it?"

Holly blew out a sigh and held Abby's stare. She hadn't planned on telling Lucy about her evening, partly because she didn't want to think about it herself. Recounting the details would only conjure up images of Max's handsome face so close to hers, his strong, broad arm around her shoulder, that irresistible grin, and those were thoughts she couldn't afford to have.

"I didn't want to make a big deal out of it," she told Lucy with a shrug.

"Well, I am making a big deal out of it," said Abby.

"I noticed." Holly picked up her hot chocolate and took a tentative sip to test the temperature.

"Am I missing something here?" Lucy asked, eyes darting from one woman to the next and back again. "I met that man—Max, right? You should be shouting from the rooftops, my girl! Why aren't you more excited?"

Holly's shoulders slumped and she toyed with the lid of her cup. "I just don't want to fall for him. He's leaving in a matter of days, and I don't think he wants anything more than a fling."

Abby peered at her. "What makes you say that?"

Holly tried to remember Max's exact words but her thoughts were muddled with a devastating image of his smooth grin and dazzling blue eyes. "He said that he doesn't have time for much in his life besides work, essentially. It just...it just felt like Brendan all over again."

"Holly." Abby's voice was stern. "Max is not Brendan. Just because Brendan disappointed you in the end doesn't mean that Max will, too. They are completely different people and the circumstances are, too. Max deserves a fair shot. It isn't right to judge him based on your past experiences."

Holly's heart sank as she listened to her friend's lecture. "No, you're right. But at the same time, tell me exactly how this would even work? He is a self-diagnosed workaholic. He lives two hours away. He has an aversion to small-town life. And oh, he hates Christmas."

Abby and Lucy gasped simultaneously. "He hates Christmas?" Abby hissed.

Holly nodded her head victoriously, satisfied in a twisted sort of way that she had managed to prove her point to them. Max was all wrong for her. She would be a fool to fall for him.

Ever the pragmatic one, Lucy clarified, "Does he just not celebrate Christmas, or does he actually hate it?"

"He hates it!" Holly's voice was shrill with defense, hoping for any reason to validate why Max was all wrong for her and why she should be allowed to just forget him. She met Lucy's suspicious gaze and added, "He said it isn't his thing."

"But who hates Christmas?" Abby asked again.

Holly threw up her hands. "Exactly!" But even as she said it, she couldn't shake the rest of his words from her thoughts. Christmas brought back bad memories, he'd said. A feeling she knew all too well.

She would never forget the first Christmas after her parents had died. First the dread leading up to it, then the incessant ache in her heart and finally the relief she had felt the next day, when it was all over. She'd feared ever having to spend another holiday that way—raw with hurt and an overwhelming sense of loss.

She set her jaw. Well, she never had again. Christmas was a busy and happy time. That's the way it was meant to be. It was better that way.

She let out a shaky sigh and began frantically arranging her jam jars in a pyramid, realizing the other two women were watching her carefully. She glanced up at one of the accusers. "What?"

"Who cares if he hates Christmas," Lucy said. "A man that looks like that is allowed to hate anything he wants."

Abby laughed heartily and took a sip of her cocoa. "Seriously, Holly. You're just talking yourself out of this with one flimsy excuse after another. It's okay to like him, you know."

"I know," Holly said halfheartedly, feeling lightheaded

over it all. The thought of allowing herself to indulge in these feelings was so far outside her comfort zone she almost couldn't bear it. She had spent years creating this cozy, safe environment for herself, and now everything felt uncertain again. She didn't know why, but she had an uneasy sensation that everything was about to fall out from under her. That Max's arrival had permanently shattered her comfortable, complacent life.

"You sure you know?" Lucy asked. "Because that face looks like it needs some persuading."

Believe me, Holly thought, *I don't need any persuading at all.*

And that was half the problem.

"What if he goes back to New York next week and I never see him again?" Holly voiced. Saying it out loud felt good, like a weight had been lifted. She was so tired of loving people only to have them leave her one way or another in the end. There was nothing more painful than being left behind. She'd much prefer to be the one leaving first for a change.

"I've got a few years on you, so let me give you a piece of advice, Holly. Anyone who disappears from your life isn't worth having in it." Lucy gave her a hard stare from under the hood of her lids.

The corner of Holly's mouth turned in a small smile. "You're a good friend, Lucy."

"Don't you forget it." Lucy winked.

"Well, speak of the devil," Abby murmured and Holly's heart skipped a beat.

Across the town square, Max was weaving his way through the stalls, stopping every few feet to pause at a cart. At the mere sight of him, Holly's stomach dropped and a wave of nausea engulfed her.

Lovesick, she thought bitterly.

There was really no point in fighting the inevitable. She was smitten. And who could blame her?

She watched him through the crowd until he disappeared behind the massive Christmas tree in the middle of the market. Before he could appear again, she turned herself away, planting a smile on her face when a little girl in a bright pink coat and matching hat asked for a jar of preserves.

"Five dollars," Holly said absentmindedly. She scanned the crowd quickly once more, but she couldn't spot Max or his navy blue parka anymore.

"I only have four," the little girl said.

Heart pounding, Holly's eyes swept over the Christmas Market once more, wondering if he had come to find her, and if so, what he wanted to say. Perhaps he had already left.

"Take it. That's fine," she said, handing the little girl a jar with barely another glance.

"If you keep running your business like that, you'll go broke." At the sound of his voice, Holly jumped. "Sorry to startle you." His deep, smooth voice sent a warm rush through Holly's blood. Her heart reeled.

Turning to face him, she swallowed hard before saying, "What a nice surprise."

"Thought I'd come see what all the fuss was about," he said. He was holding a small brown paper bag full of roasted chestnuts and he popped a few in his mouth as he looked around the town square.

Holly could feel the heat of Lucy's stare boring into her from the next cart. She mentally dismissed it as she studied Max's profile. Every inch of it was perfect, from the loose lock of dark hair that spilled over his forehead to the strong nose to the square jaw. "I didn't think this would be your kind of thing."

Max lifted a mischievous brow. "I'm a man full of surprises," he bantered and Holly gave a weak smile.

Beside her, Abby cleared her throat and Holly jolted. Squaring her shoulders she said, "Max, I don't think you've officially met Abby yet."

Max took off his glove and held out his hand. "I've seen you around the inn. And Holly's mentioned you a few times, as well."

"Nice to meet you, *Max,*" Abby said, with more meaning than Holly cared for. "I've seen you around the inn, but you were always being snatched away by Evelyn Adler before I could introduce myself."

Max chuckled. "Will you be back at the inn today?'

Holly stiffened as Abby said, "No, Holly here was nice enough to give me the week off since everyone's gone home. Guess she figures she can handle you on her own."

Max slid his blazing blue eyes to Holly and held them there. The corner of his lips lifted in a lazy smile. "I might be more trouble than she expected."

Holly felt her cheeks color a shade of pink she didn't even want to envision. Under the cart, where Max couldn't see, she gave Abby a less than gentle kick with the toe of her boot. Abby turned to her with a frozen smile, but her eyes were warm and dancing. She was enjoying herself. Of course. Easy for her, being married already. Not having to put herself out there. Risk her heart.

But she couldn't stay mad at Abby. Not really. Abby was her closest friend and she wanted what was best for her. And it seemed everyone around Holly thought what was best for her was Max Hamilton.

"So how do you like Maple Woods?" Abby inquired, because Holly was sure, she simply couldn't resist.

"It's quaint!" Max said heartily, his smile open and genuine. He slipped a glove back on his hand; his nose and cheeks were turning pink with cold.

"Well, hopefully you'll stick around," Abby said. "At least long enough to cover my spot." She stepped away from the cart. Would you mind? I have to go find my husband."

If Max was opposed to the suggestion, he didn't show it, and he swiftly stepped behind the cart once Abby had shuffled out. Before any excuse could be made from anyone, she darted into the crowd, her hand-knitted scarf flying behind her until she disappeared into the swarm of people.

Holly bit her lip to hide its smile.

"So what are you selling here?" Max held up a jar and studied the label. She'd printed them up herself with The White Barn Inn logo, as well as tied a twine bow around the bottom of each parchment-paper covered lid. "Wild Blueberry Preserves," he read.

"From the bushes out back," she said quietly.

"The bushes that witnessed Evelyn Adler's breakdown one afternoon?" He cocked a brow and looked at her sidelong.

Holly laughed. "The very same ones."

Max studied the jar once more before setting it back on the display table. "Let me guess. You made them."

"Is it that obvious?" she sighed.

"More like that impressive," he corrected and her heart flipped at the compliment. "You've got everyone here fooled into thinking you're perfect. But luckily I happen to know your dirty little secret."

Holly gasped. "What's that?"

"That you are the world's worst waitress. Hostess. Barista. Cashier."

At the stall next to them, Lucy snorted with mirth.

"You're never going to let that one go, are you?" Holly asked, searching his handsome face.

"Nope." He grinned ear-to-ear and took another handful of chestnuts out of the bag.

"I should have known better than to tell you that story," Holly said ruefully, but she couldn't help but laugh at herself.

"Hi, Lucy," Max said, holding up his hand to the neighboring stall.

Lucy smiled, "Pleasure to see you again. What do you think of our little Christmas Market?"

"Never seen anything like it," he said. "Usually I'm too busy to notice these types of things."

Holly flashed Lucy a pointed look and then swiftly returned to her task. She scanned the crowd for Abby, who was standing near the tree talking to Pete and gesturing back toward the stand.

"You mean too busy to notice the holidays?" Lucy was asking Max.

"Guess you could say that. It's pretty hard to avoid it here, though."

His smile didn't waver but Holly bristled at his word choice. Why would he want to avoid the holidays? What bad memories did it conjure up for him?

"Well, I'm excited for Christmas this year," Holly announced, lifting her chin.

"Holly, you're excited for Christmas every year." Lucy chuckled.

Not every year, Holly thought darkly.

She steeled herself, forcing herself back to the present. "Well, this year is different."

"And why is that?" Max popped another chestnut in his mouth and chewed, his eyes clasped on hers as he waited for her answer.

"Because this is the Christmas I finally get my inn," she said, glancing to Lucy, who smiled.

"Aw, honey. I'm so happy for you," she said. "It's been a long time coming. I know this holiday is a special one for you."

Despite the chill in the air, Holly felt a warm flood wash over her. Every time she stopped to remember that in only a matter of days the inn would be hers, she felt the same flicker of excitement mixed with relief.

She knew the inn had always been hers in spirit. The Millers had never put any demands or restrictions on the land or its uses. They had inherited the land in the same fashion she had inherited the lease, and with it being leased to the Tate family for coming up on ninety-nine years, most people in town didn't even know Holly didn't own it outright. For as long as anyone could remember, some generation of the Tates had lived in the old mansion her great-grandfather had built on rented land. It was her home, and George and Lucy treated it as such.

But that didn't keep Holly from wanting to make it official.

She'd had too many close calls in life. Too many times where she thought something was a sure bet, only to discover that everything she had poured her heart and soul into could be taken at a moment's notice. And without warning.

Beside her Max was surprisingly quiet.

"Everything okay?" she asked and he shrugged his response. She shifted uncomfortably from one foot to the other, racking her mind for what could have caused this transition in his mood. "If you need to get back, the inn is open. You can come and go as you please," she offered.

"You just left the door *open?*" Max was immediately pulled from his brooding mood. His eyes flinched as they bore into hers and his brows met in the middle.

Holly stopped to register the question and laughed softly when she realized how trusting this must seem. When she had first moved here from Boston, she never would have dreamed of doing such a thing; if anything, she had been scared living alone in that giant house. Everywhere she turned was a shadow of something past, a memory of something that was long gone. She had certainly changed a lot in five years, she mused, but some things did remain the same.

She hated being alone in that house. It was much better when it was filled with people. It would be even better if it was filled with her own family, too.

"We're all friends in Maple Woods," she said easily.

"So," he said, leaning in closer to her once more. Her pulse quickened as she waited for his next words. "If you told Stephen and Abby to take the week off, did you do the same with the rest of the staff?"

"Yes."

"So it's just you and me, alone in that house?"

Her heart plummeted. "Yes," she said slowly, not daring to say much more, and a slight smile formed at the corners of her lips. She glanced at him sidelong, catching the flash of the electric blue of his eyes piercing hers.

"So that means no cook again tonight?"

Holly furrowed her brow. "No, but I can make something."

Max grinned. "Not if I can help it."

Holly looked up at him quizzically. "Excuse me?"

"I'm making dinner tonight. For both of us. Unless you have other plans, that is?"

Holly chuckled, unsure of how to handle the flirtatious look in his sparkling blue eyes. She had never before encountered a man so confident in his approach. His gorgeous face was only enhanced by the powerful way he commanded their situation. He wasn't going to take no for an answer, she realized.

Not that she was arguing.

* * *

Max wasn't sure what he was doing, but frankly, he didn't care. He knew what he *should* do: walk away. Today. Now. He should get in his car and drive back to New York. He should be gone by the time Holly got back to the inn that night.

What he wanted to do, however, was vastly different.

He was fairly sure that the inn's kitchen was stocked with more food than he would need, but just in case, he decided to stop in the local grocery for the ingredients he would need for the dinner he had decided to make. The thought of going back to that inn by himself bothered him. He had become fond of being surrounded by the cheerful din of guests, and he had to admit it saddened him to think that Evelyn wouldn't be knocking on his door at some point today.

A sharp stab halted his breath when he realized the domino effect of the events he had set into action. Evelyn Adler depended on The White Barn Inn to give her a special Christmas each year. And he was single-handedly taking that from her.

She was an older woman, with only her husband to keep her company. What would she do next year? And what would Holly do?

Not for the first time since his meeting with George Miller, Max had to physically restrain himself from marching straight back to the Miller cottage and rescinding his offer. But he knew that as much as he wished he could do this, it wasn't exactly an option, unless he was willing to sacrifice everything else in his life.

And he had worked too hard and come too far to do that. If he took back his offer on the land, there would be no new development, and from there it would be only a matter of time before they'd have to merge or sell to a competitor, as so many rivals had already done. This development was his road to recovery—it would offset the revenue loss and keep his options open.

If he didn't build on this land, he didn't build at all, it was that simple. None of the anchors would take a gamble on weak demographics any more than Hamilton Properties would, and the research for this project was rock solid. Sales projections were strong. He couldn't risk letting the major retailers down now. He was depending on them as much as they were him. If he didn't deliver this project and they started pulling out of other centers…it wouldn't be long before everything unraveled.

His life's work. Gone. He couldn't bear to think about it.

"Mr. Hamilton."

Max darted his gaze to the left, where Bobby Miller was seated on a bench outside the grocery store. "I don't remember telling you my name," he said, walking closer.

Bobby shrugged. "You're the first new face we've seen here in ages. Everyone knows your name."

Max did a quick mental calculation of how many hours had passed since he'd left the Miller cottage. Long enough for George to have said something to his son, or for Bobby to have overheard something he shouldn't have.

"What have you been up to today?" he inquired, studying Bobby's face for any insight into what the kid might know.

Bobby shoved his hands in his pockets. "Just hanging out with my friends," he said. "There's not much to do around this town."

Unsatisfied with his answer, Max probed further. "I met your dad last night at the diner. He's a nice guy."

Bobby gazed at him warily. "If you say so," he said at last.

"What's he up to today?" Max asked.

"Beats me. Probably working. I haven't seen him."

Max let out a long sigh of relief. "Well, I should be going. It was good seeing you again, Bobby."

Bobby waved his hand unenthusiastically as Max pressed on. As he rounded the corner to the automatic doors of the store, a pungent whiff of cigarette smoke cut through the fresh country air and caught Max's attention. He turned his head reflexively, but there was no offender in sight. Out of curiosity, he poked his head back around the corner of the building, but Bobby was already gone and the smell of smoke had already started to fade.

Still shaky from the exchange, he forced himself to concentrate on the dinner ahead with Holly as he pulled one item after another off the shelves of the quaint store and tucked them into his basket. Rounding to the produce section, he looked up and locked eyes with Mayor Pearson.

The older man shifted his eyes from the left to the right before walking slowly over to Max. "Good to see you again, Mayor," Max said.

The quizzical expression on his face must have been apparent for the mayor explained, "The office is closed on weekends and I've got a new assignment for this afternoon." He tilted his basket to reveal several boxes of candy canes. "I've been cast in the starring role in Santa's Village. Right down to the fat suit." He offered a dry smile. "If you haven't noticed, Christmas is a big deal in our little town."

Max widened his eyes at the obvious. "I've just come from the Christmas Market, actually."

The mayor spared a wry smile. "It's a cheerful time for everyone, which is why I hate the thought of disrupting the spirit. Do you mind me asking where things stand on the matter we discussed yesterday? Has any progress been made?"

Max nodded his head slowly. Lowering his voice, he said, "I met with George Miller this morning."

"And?"

"He's asked for some time to consider the offer, but seemed receptive."

Mayor Pearson raised his brows. "Did he say when he would give you his answer?"

Max shook his head. "He needs to discuss it with his wife first, but he knows that time is of the essence. He promised he would have an answer to me with ample time to put the project before the planning committee."

The mayor leaned in and asked, "Does anyone else know?"

"No," Max's tone was firm. Of this much, he was certain. His moment of paranoia had been a fleeting lapse. When he stopped to think about the overwhelming ramifications of the proposal, he knew that George Miller wouldn't say a word to anyone but his wife. This was a tight-knit community. Word of something of this magnitude getting out would have a disastrous ripple effect on everyone.

His stomach tightened. Was George Miller really ready to put himself in the middle of a firing squad? Max hadn't stopped to think about the impact the local outcry might have on the diner. But then, with the amount of money the Millers would reap, they wouldn't need to rely on their customers anymore.

"What about Holly?" the mayor pressed.

"What about her?" Max was quick to reply. The mere mention of her name prompted him to rush to defense. But who was he protecting? Himself…or her?

"Does she know that you have made an offer to George?"

"No," Max said, feeling disgusted with himself. "I

thought about talking with her about it, but I get the impression she wouldn't be happy about this."

"That's an understatement," the mayor said. He shook his head. "I've been up all night thinking about this, but ultimately one person can't hold the rest of the town back from progress. Holly is sitting on something that can be put to better use, and that's the way I have to approach this." He sighed. "Who knows, maybe if that library hadn't caught fire I would be saying something different."

Max paused to think about this last statement. If the idea of building on the Miller site had never been possible, would that have been better? Then he could have just enjoyed his time with Holly for what it was. Because where he stood now, one thing was inevitable: in a matter of days—if not hours—Holly would learn his real reason for being in Maple Woods.

And then she would hate him.

The thought of her feeling betrayed by him was almost too much to bear. Especially when he himself wished it didn't have to be this way. Tonight he would try and tell her the truth. Cooking dinner was the least he could do for her, in light of everything else.

"I suppose I should get going," the mayor said, starting to walk away. "But I have a feeling we'll be in touch soon."

"It was good seeing you again, Mayor."

"Talk to you soon, Mr. Hamilton." The mayor made his departure, and Max quietly watched him disappear down an aisle until the man was out of sight.

A domino effect, he thought to himself once more. That's exactly what it was. He had knocked the first chip yesterday morning, and now there was no chance of him halting the breaks without it all crashing down on him anyway. If he at least let the plan stay in motion, it had a chance of falling neatly into a pile.

And why was he even questioning his actions anyway?

This was what he had wanted. This was what he had worked for. This was what he had come to town to do. And then he had met Holly.

And now…now he didn't know what he wanted anymore. All he knew was that he had the sickening feeling he was going to come out of all of this with nothing.

Max turned to pull some pears from a bushel against a wall and his heart pitched at what he saw.

Standing only a few feet from him was Abby, staring at him intensely, her gaze steady and lethal. The friendly smile was gone from her small face, her eyes clouded with confusion. How much she had overheard, he didn't know. She looked away hastily and was gone before he could say anything to stop her.

Chapter Eight

A loud clanging of pots and pans greeted Holly as she made her way into the warm, heavenly scented kitchen a few hours later. For a fleeting second she wondered if she should have allowed Max into her kitchen. If he damaged one of Stephen's prized sauté pans, the wrath she would face from the chef would be fierce.

Oh, well. A small price to pay for such an attractive invitation.

Holly nervously ran her hands through her long, thick hair. After returning from the Christmas Market, she'd managed to duck inside through her personal entrance at the back of the house to shower and dress. She wanted to arrive in the kitchen as she would for any other intimate evening. Even if it wasn't a date. Technically.

She had no idea what Max had planned for the night or what his intentions even were. She had a feeling that tonight would be a turning point, but maybe that was just wishful thinking.

Max stood at the stove, stirring a creamy sauce with one hand and adding handfuls of dried pasta to a boiling pot of water with the other. He set his culinary skills to the side when he saw her, greeting her with a hundred-watt smile.

"Hello there," he said and Holly felt her heart pool into something warm and thick that spread through her body like melted chocolate.

"Hi," she managed, unable to pull her eyes from him. She stood awkwardly in the doorway, never having felt so out of place in her own kitchen and resisting the urge to push up her sleeves and tie on an apron.

"Wine?" he asked rhetorically, as he filled two glasses from a decanter. Holly accepted hers with a smile and clinked his glass before taking a sip. It was smooth and rich. Perfect. He flashed her a lazy grin and Holly's pulse quickened with longing.

"So, what's for dinner?" she asked in a forced casual tone, settling herself onto a counter stool that lent an excellent vantage point to Max's activities.

"Penne with vodka sauce," he said as he picked up a dish towel and bent down to pluck a loaf of steaming, crusty bread from the oven. His back was wide and strong. Holly indulged herself in a long stare at Max's broad shoulders straining against the confines of his shirt, imagining what it would be like to stroke his bare skin with the tips of her fingers, and explore every inch of his raw, masculine physique...

She immediately gave herself a silent scolding. If she kept up this type of thinking, there was no telling where the night would end.

She'd left the Christmas Market with a new sense of hope. Talking with Lucy and Abby always made her feel better, and confiding her fears in them this morning had put her mind at ease. They were right; she was coming up with one excuse after another to keep herself from falling for Max and she was dangerously close to letting a chance for real love pass her by as a result. Practicalities aside, she had a connection with Max that she couldn't deny any longer. She had come to a point where she had to risk her heart again; if she didn't, how would she ever find that true love she so desperately wanted?

She hadn't been this attracted to a man in as long as she could remember, if ever. There was something about Max— his quiet strength mixed with a touch of vulnerability made her want to squeeze him close and never let him go. It was as if he had been brought here just for her. The realization that she could have gone through life never feeling this way, never knowing him, was fast becoming inconceivable.

"Where'd you learn to cook?" she asked, taking another sip of her wine.

"Oh, you learn a lot of things when you've been single as long as I have." Max grinned. "Like how to make your bed. Do laundry. Do the dishes."

"Very funny," Holly chided, but she smiled. "In all seriousness, you really seem to know your way around a kitchen."

"I have a weakness for cooking shows," he said. "Makes for good background noise."

Holly squinted with interest. "I take it you live alone then?"

"Always have," Max said mildly.

Deciding to go for it, Holly took a deep breath. "Do you prefer it that way?" she ventured.

Max threw her a noncommittal shrug. "Never really thought about it," he said, but something in his tone was unconvincing.

Unsatisfied, Holly toyed with the stem of her glass. Not willing to relinquish the topic just yet, she blurted, "I hate living alone," and then lowered her eyes, instantly realizing how reckless her declaration had been.

If Max was put off, he didn't show it. "I figured that was the case," he said as he stirred the sauce.

"Why?"

"You run an inn," he said. "It would be a bit inconvenient for you to have all these people in your house everyday if you preferred them not to be there."

Holly laughed at his logic. "Good point."

"So you like what you do then? Running the inn? Taking care of people day after day?"

"I love it!" she exclaimed.

"It never gets tiring?" He was watching her carefully, leaning back against the counter and clutching his wineglass.

Holly shook her head slowly. "No…I guess some days can be long, but I'm sure that's the case with any job."

Max's hooded stare held hers until she squirmed under the scrutiny. "Guess so," he said, finally releasing his hold on her to return to the pots on the stove.

What was that all about? Holly wondered. But while the topic remained on work, she decided to use it to her advantage.

"How about you?" she asked. "Do you like your job?"

"I do," he said.

She waited, but he didn't elaborate. "What do you do exactly?"

His strong, wide shoulders heaved slightly. He stopped stirring the sauce for a fraction of a second before resuming. "Real estate," he said.

Holly wasn't sure what she had been expecting to hear, but she felt inexplicable relief. He had been so cryptic about the business that was keeping him in town that her mind had started to needlessly reel with sinister possibilities.

Real estate. It probably was something to do with the library. Or maybe—a sudden thought caused Holly's hopes to soar—maybe he was planning to purchase something in Maple Woods? Her heart began to thump with the implications. Any kind of real estate investment that he was making would surely bring him back to Maple Woods often. If not permanently. She didn't know much about real estate, but she had reason to hope, at least.

Barely managing to hide her bursting smile, Holly took another sip of wine and watched as Max continued his cooking efforts. "It smells delicious," she observed.

Max turned and flashed her a grin over his shoulder. "Thanks. Hopefully it tastes good, too." He plated the pasta and turned to face her. "Dinner is served."

The fire was roaring in the lobby and the tree twinkled invitingly as she followed Max into the dimly lit room. He set the tray down on the coffee table and without a word, sunk into the sofa next to her. A stir of excitement ran down her spine.

This was cozy.

Max held up his wine glass. "To…chance meetings."

Holly stomach tightened as she clinked his glass with hers and took a long, delicious sip. She knew by sitting here like this, it would be harder than ever to back out of… whatever this was.

Her mind began to race with possibilities.

Watching him over the rim of her glass, Holly wasn't sure how much longer she could hold back. In the few days she had been with him, her heart had felt something foreign and wonderful. Something seemed to click and tell her this was right despite how much she had desperately tried to convince herself otherwise. It was only a doubtful corner of her mind that told her to fight what her heart so desperately wanted.

Didn't any real love involve a risk or sacrifice?

"This is delicious," Holly commented, taking a bite of the warm, creamy pasta.

"I'm a man of many talents, believe it or not," Max joked and that adorable grin came over his mouth.

"Oh, yeah? What other tricks do you have under your belt? I'd like to see what you're keeping down there." As soon as the words were out, Holly felt the color drain from her face. Max's eyes burst open in surprise, and his expression froze until his lips began to twitch.

Holly tittered nervously but Max's sudden roar of laughter muffled her own feeble sounds. She slid her pasta around her plate, unable to eat from humiliation and wondering what exactly Max would say when he had finally settled down. She furiously scrambled for a delicate way to change the subject.

"Sorry," she settled on. "That didn't come out right."

Max's eyes were sharp in their hold on hers. "Darn, I was hoping it came out exactly right."

Holly's cheeks burned with heat and she knew this time the flush didn't go unnoticed. She forced a bit of food into her mouth and chewed slowly, barely able to swallow due to the knot that had formed in her throat.

Needing physical distance, she set her plate on the table and crossed the room without a word. With the press of a button, soft music poured through the speakers and broke up the silence.

From afar, Holly could see Max's brow furrow. She immediately knew why.

"Christmas carols," she said. "What can I say? 'Tis the season."

Taking in the large lobby—from the stockings over the

crackling fire to the enormous tree, to the garland wrapped around the banister in the adjacent foyer—Holly thought back on her conversation with Max the day before. "I hope all this doesn't offend you," she said, hoping she wasn't being insensitive.

"It doesn't offend me. It's just—"

"Not your thing," Holly finished, managing a wry smile.

Max matched her expression. "Does that bother you?"

Holly fell back onto her cushion next to Max and studied his face. "No," she said honestly. "It just makes me curious. And a little sad," she added softly.

Perhaps it was the wine, perhaps it was the warmth from the flames flickering in hearth, perhaps it was the damn music...or perhaps it was just Holly. Sweet, beautiful Holly. Max didn't know the reason, but for the first time in years, he felt at peace.

"I think I told you the first night we met that I grew up in a small town like this." His voice was low and husky, his eyes firmly on the fire.

"I remember," Holly said softly. She waited, patient for him to continue.

Max took another forkful of pasta and chewed, his mind in two places at once. Here in the safety of this homey room, and back in his childhood home. Which was hardly a home at all.

"It was awful," he blurted.

Holly raised a questioning brow. "Small-town life?"

"All of it." He grimaced at the memories. A series of images he had pushed aside. A life he had put behind him.

Holly's brow furrowed in concern. "What was so terrible?"

"My mom got pregnant with me out of wedlock when she was...very young. It was a scandal, especially back in those days, and the small-town lifestyle didn't help matters."

Holly frowned. "That would be hard."

Max nodded and watched the flames grow in the fireplace. "She had so many things she wanted to do with her life," he mused. Turning to Holly he said, "She was a musician. A singer, actually. And a very good one. She had a music scholarship to college."

"Impressive," Holly said but Max shook his head to show she had misunderstood.

"She couldn't go."

He met Holly's gaze. Her eyes flickered in realization. Her lids drooped slightly until she lowered her eyes, her long black lashes skimming her cheeks.

"Because—"

"Because of me." Max nodded.

"That must have been hard," Holly said quietly.

"More than you know," Max said as a swell of resentment built inside him and turned his heart heavy. "It was as if, all my life, I could sense this unhappiness in her. This longing to be somewhere else. Doing something else. And there was nothing I could do to make her happy."

"But couldn't she pursue her music in another way?" Holly asked. "Could she teach at school or give private lessons?"

Max shook his head. It wasn't just about the music, which represented everything she wanted and didn't have—couldn't have. His gut twisted when he thought how different his mother's life might have been if he had never been born. But when he grew older—and, after everything happened—he knew that she had made her choice. She had done the best she could. She had thought she could make it work. She just…couldn't.

"For a long time, when I was very little, she would walk

around the house singing." A faint smile tugged at the corner of his mouth at the memory of his mother, so young then, in a housedress and apron, standing over a sink of dirty dishes crooning Sinatra and old show tunes like there was an audience in the living room just waiting to throw roses at her bare feet. "I remember sitting on that old linoleum in our kitchen playing with my toy cars and just listening to that voice…no sweeter sound."

Holly smiled and locked her eyes with him, encouraging him to continue.

"Sometimes, when I was about two or three, she'd turn on the record player and just dance around the house, singing, holding my hands, twirling me around…and the next thing I knew, she'd stop and just burst into tears. And I never understood it."

"That's so sad," Holly murmured, her voice cracking.

Max forced a smile. The last thing he needed was Holly thinking he was feeling sorry for himself. Once he might have, but not anymore. Time had a way of fading the rawness of pain, even if it didn't always heal the wounds.

"And your father? Was he around?" Holly said the words hesitantly, as if not sure she should be asking.

Max emitted a deep sigh. "They got married when my mother was pregnant," he said and before Holly's expression could shift any further in the direction of hope he added, "It was the worst decision my mother could have made."

Holly's hazel eyes shot open in surprise and then crinkled as her brows met in the center. "How so?"

"He was the town drunk," Max said simply. He clenched his jaw, all sadness evaporating at the thought of his father. There was no place in his heart for that man. Any time he happened to think of him, ice filled his chest. "I just remember that night after night, he would come home late, sometimes when I was already in bed, reeking of booze, stumbling around, crashing into lamps, and he and my mother would just *scream* at each other. For hours." Max chuckled. "I tried putting cotton in my ears, and one time it got stuck. My mother had to take me to the doctor to fish it out."

He slid a glance at Holly. She gave a watery smile. "You didn't have any brothers and sisters?"

"No."

"Me, neither."

He wasn't sure why, but something about this shared bond made him feel closer to her. Even if—judging from this place—her circumstances had been quite different than his own.

"Money was always tight," he continued. "Especially around the holidays. My dad spent all the money he made at the mill on booze at the town bar after work. More than a few times a week my mom would get a phone call from the owner of the tavern, telling her to come collect him, that he was too drunk to drive home. She'd have to ask the lady next door to come sit with me. I'll never forget the shame in her face. Or the fear in her eyes."

"She was afraid of him?" Holly asked gently.

"My father was a mean drunk," Max said. "A mean, mean drunk. When he got like that…my mother didn't know what she was about to step into. She walked on glass. As did I."

"Did he ever hurt her? Or—" Holly paused as the horrifying thought took hold, but Max waved away her concern with his hand.

"He never hurt either of us. Nah, he preferred to punish my mother in other ways."

"But why?"

Max shrugged. "For trapping him. For getting pregnant with me. He was miserable."

"But she didn't do it on purpose!" Holly protested.

"Oh, I know. But he didn't care." Max swallowed when he thought about the truth in Holly's statement. She hadn't meant to be hurtful, but the words cut him to the bone. She was right. His mother hadn't gotten pregnant on purpose. He hadn't been planned. *Or wanted.*

"But what did he do then? To punish her?"

Max felt almost grateful that Holly was asking so many questions. It made opening up to her so much easier. She sensed his need to tell her this—to finally talk about it. That was what made Holly so easy to approach, he realized. She didn't just feign an interest in people's lives. She genuinely cared.

"Oh…he would break things that were special to her. He always apologized once he'd sobered up, but some things couldn't be replaced."

"Like her record player?" Holly ventured.

Man, she was good. "Yep," Max said with a bitter smile. "And since money was tight, she never got another."

Holly frowned, her eyes holding his almost pleadingly. "Is that when she stopped singing?"

Max sighed deeply. "No, she stopped long before that. Around the house, at least. You asked about her giving music lessons? She did that once."

"Just once? What happened?"

Max swallowed hard. "Remember how I told you about that train I wanted for Christmas one year?" Holly nodded and Max continued, "I never connected it until much later, but she took a job giving singing lessons to a girl in town. A daughter of one of her friends from high school."

"That was the only time?" Holly was squinting at him, trying to piece the nuggets of information together.

"She isolated herself over time," he explained. "You know how it is living here in this small town. Everyone knows you. Everyone knows your business. It's fine when you have nothing to hide, but when you do, it can be really tough. People would whisper when she'd take me to the store—some just loving the gossip, some feeling pity—and her face…I just remember the look on her face. The way she would hang her head. The way she wouldn't make eye contact. The way the light in her eyes was just gone. It just became too much for her."

And for me too, he thought.

Holly shifted her eyes to the fire. "That would be very hard," she reflected. "Small-town life isn't always easy."

"No, and in this case, it was impossible. Everyone knew my father. And everyone heard the screaming."

Holly grimaced. "That must have been difficult to listen to every day."

"You get used to it. What other choice do you have?"

"Did your mother every think about leaving?"

Max leaned forward and stoked the fire. "That year when I asked for the train, she gave music lessons twice a week to save for that train. Two days before Christmas, my father found the money. They had a terrible fight. I was too young to understand at the time. Heck." He chuckled. "I still believed in Santa."

Holly eyes searched his. "What happened?"

"He spent all the money my mom had earned on a round of beers for his buddies down at the tavern," he said simply.

"The money for the train," Holly summarized quietly.

Max shrugged. "The next day, she was gone. No train. No mother. Nothing under the tree. And that," he said, "is when I stopped believing."

Holly wiped away a tear with the back of her hand and let her gaze drift to the fire. They lapsed into silence, watching the flames crackle and dance. Eventually she asked, "Did you ever see her again?"

Max inhaled deeply. "She said she'd be back for me once she found a job and had a place for us."

Holly gave him a measured look, already knowing the ending to the story. "But she never came back."

"No."

"Did you ever try to find her?"

"I went looking for her when I moved to New York. I thought she might have gotten into some off-Broadway show, that type of thing. But there was no trace of her." He paused. "She probably changed her name."

She wanted to start fresh. Just like I eventually did, he thought.

"And your father?"

"I left that town when I was eighteen and never looked back," he said firmly. "No reason to."

Silence fell over the room until Holly finally spoke. "I am so sorry, Max."

He turned to her, shrugging dismissively to curtail the enormity of what he had just told her. "I survived."

Beside him, Holly remained solemn. "It isn't fair."

"Who said life has to be fair?" he asked. He reached for his plate, pleased to find the food was still warm from the heat of the fire.

"It would be nice if it could be," Holly said, giving him a thin smile.

His stare held hers as he took a the last bite of pasta and set the empty plate back on the table. It was a comforting feeling, to be under her protective gaze, and when her hand slid over to tentatively graze his, he grasped for it, squeezing it in his large palm and feeling more connected to her in that moment than he ever had with anyone before her.

"Should we have our dessert now?" Holly forced a cheerful smile as she eyed Max cautiously, gauging his mood.

Her own heart still ached when she thought of the story he had shared. She could only imagine how he must feel. Unless it was something that was so much a part of him it didn't touch him in the same way anymore.

Max smiled in relief. "What's on the menu?"

Holly hesitated. "Oh. You didn't—" She'd assumed he had made the final course, but the expectant look on his face told her otherwise. She smiled to herself. The inn-keeper in her wanted to scold him, but his oversight only endeared him to her.

"How about pie?" she suggested. He was still her guest, after all.

"Sounds great," Max said, standing to help her load the tray.

Holly watched him carefully as he went about the menial task. Max didn't open up easily from what she'd gotten to know of him so far, but for some reason, he had chosen to share his innermost thoughts with her tonight. The look of loss and pain in his eyes when he spoke of his childhood tore at Holly's heartstrings. She felt a stab in the gut as she looked around at the festive decorations, wondering what kind of painful reminder they might be causing him.

Once they would have hurt her, too.

"Do you want me to take down the tree?" she blurted.

Max's bright blue eyes flung open. "What? Why?"

Holly shifted uncomfortably from one foot to the next, looking desperately from the tree back to Max. "I under-stand now why Christmas is a difficult time for you. I don't want to do anything to make it worse."

Max's eyes softened as he threw her a lopsided, boyish smile and Holly felt her stomach flutter. God help her. She wasn't sure how much longer she could resist him. As it was he consumed her every thought when she wasn't with him. And when she was...

"The truth is that I normally don't spend this much time with women who listen to Christmas carols or bake gingerbread houses," he said, motioning to the candy house perched on an end table.

Holly's frowned in. So there it was. She wasn't his type. Just as she had suspected. "Oh."

She glanced up to see Max's mouth curl into a smile. He took a step toward her, and she felt her body stiffen at his nearness. Their eyes were locked, each looking to the other to make sense of the situation.

"And you probably aren't used to spending so much time with someone who would rather ignore Christmas."

"Well, no—" Holly shook her head in protestation, but her words were lost as Max dipped his chin, lowering his mouth to hers.

"I'm willing to make an exception if you are," he murmured. His fingers traced the curve of her waist, lingering just above her hip. She shifted with desire and twisted her body closer to his.

His face was so close to hers, she could feel the heat of his breath, catch the scent of musk on his skin. His eyes flamed with hunger and Holly shuddered in anticipation. His lips met hers once again, grazing them gently at first and then opening to explore her further. Her stiff, shocked body slowly relaxed in his arms, and she felt herself giving in to him as his strong, determined hands pulled her body against his own.

Max's tongue danced slowly with hers, and then adjusted its rhythm as he sensed her arousal, probing her in a way that caused her knees to go weak.

Dropping the napkin she'd been holding on to for dear life, she pressed herself closer to him. His chest was firm and tight and she could feel the hard planes of his muscles through the thin material of his shirt. She slid her hand farther up his strong, wide back, taking in the contours of his broad torso, the heat emanating from his skin. She molded herself into him, pressing the swell of her breasts against his body, breathing in his masculine scent. A mixture of soap or aftershave, it was distinct and intoxicating.

She sensed him smile before he released her lips. His breath was hot in her ear, sending a tingle down her spine.

"You know, I've been wanting to do that for days," he said, his voice low and husky.

"Why'd you wait so long?" she asked through a grin, glancing up at him.

His arms slid to her waist, his blue eyes piercing. "I could get used to that."

So could I, Holly thought.

Chapter Nine

Max tossed and turned into the early-morning hours. By four, he admitted defeat, and turned on the bedside lamp. Sleep would be impossible as long as his mind searched for a solution to ease the knot in his gut that tightened every time he imagined Holly's face when she discovered his true purpose here. He couldn't get his mind off Holly—the way her lips had felt against his, the way the soft, feminine curves of her body had made his groin tighten with arousal. There was no denying that he wanted her. He wanted to touch her, kiss her…but he couldn't think about these things now. He had to keep a level head.

Pulling out his laptop, he reviewed the materials for the umpteenth time. Everything for an impending pitch to the city planning board was in place. The financial and demographic reports were solid. The architectural renderings polished and attractive. The retail tenants that had already committed to the project were appealing and upscale, indicating others would follow. It was all there for the taking.

But for Max, the project had lost its luster.

He tried in vain to create a secondary plan, seeing if it was even feasible for the company to restore their existing projects rather than pursue new developments. But as he examined—and reexamined—the spreadsheets detailing how much money had already been poured into the planning of this new development, he knew he had to see it through. There was no denying it. If Hamilton Properties was going to stay in business, the project had to be built. It was the only thing that would save the existing centers and generate new revenue for the company.

Financially, he would be fine if Hamilton Properties went bust. But was he really thinking of sabotaging years of hard work over a woman he barely knew? A woman he knew he couldn't even have a future with...

His work—the business he had worked so hard to build from nothing, when he'd started with nothing—was his life. It represented who he was now. The obstacles he had overcome.

He would have to be a fool to just throw it all away. But would he be a bigger fool to throw Holly away?

The kiss last night had been more promising than he'd expected. Sure, Holly was pretty and sweet, but the electric bolt he'd felt as their lips explored each other was more than he could have anticipated. His mind was clouded, reeling with memories of her touch, flooded with anxiety over the fallout of this project. Time was ticking fast. And he had a bad feeling everything was about to explode.

And that he'd be the one getting burned.

Max stood up from the desk in his room and stared out the window onto the snow-covered fields that surrounded the inn. He rubbed at the stubble on his chin and thought long and hard, but his mind was blank. The White Barn Inn was sitting on a gold mine. It could be put to much better use.

Or so I keep telling myself, he thought.

Max drew a deep breath and glanced at his watch, surprised to realize that it was already almost nine. Heaving a sigh, he ran his fingers through his bedraggled hair. He'd deal with the business matters later. Surely by now Holly would be busy in the kitchen, whipping up something fragrant and delicious as she did every morning, and that was all the distraction he needed at the moment.

Besides, maybe George Miller wouldn't even accept the offer.

Max pushed the thought away as quickly as it formed. *Ludicrous.* He liked Holly...a lot. But he couldn't go throwing away a project this big based on attraction...no matter how deep.

His mind flashed to an image of Holly standing in the sun-filled kitchen in that red Christmas apron, humming carols to herself and sprinkling cinnamon into her coffee. Something inside him swelled as he recalled the sensation of her full breasts against his chest. Had that only been last night? It felt surreal now. To think he had held her in his arms. In that moment she had been all his. When he allowed his mind to wander there, he knew he couldn't let her go.

But he wasn't sure he had a choice.

Showering and shaving quickly, he dressed in one of the new sweaters he had bought in town and crossed to the door, mentally talking himself through the next part of the day. As difficult as it was going to be, he had to talk to Holly today. It was only three days until Christmas, and for all he knew, Abby had overheard too much of his conversation with the mayor. Or Bobby Miller had overheard his parents talking and told his friends. It was a small town and Max knew all too well how quickly gossip could spread.

Holly was going to learn the truth sooner rather than later anyway. It would be better if it came from him.

Now was the time to go after everything he wanted. Full force. The business and Holly.

There was no other way.

As he pulled the door to his room closed behind him and made his way down the sweeping staircase to the lobby, something told him that her attachment to the inn extended beyond it being her business or even her grandmother's home. There was something deeper keeping her here, something that might be pivotal to the situation, and he intended to figure out exactly what that was. Today.

Holly pulled a few logs of kindling from the pile stacked neatly against the back of the house and sniffed. The biting cold was already making the tip of her nose burn and her eyes tear. Clutching the firewood to her chest, she threw her head back and allowed the morning sun to wash down over her face. A fresh wave of excitement tickled her spine when she thought of seeing Max again today. It had been a long time since she had felt this powerful flush of desire, and the heat he had awakened in her kept her warm all through the night.

A tapping at the glass from the kitchen window caused her to jump. Her eyes flew open to see Max smiling at her and waving. Her heart dropped to her stomach and stayed there as she turned the handle to the mudroom and, after hanging her coat on the rack and setting her boots on the rug to dry, emerged into the warm, fragrant kitchen.

Max was leaning against the counter, already clutching a steaming mug of coffee. "Morning." He grinned sheepishly, and she smiled in return.

"Sleep well?" she asked. Unable to look him in the eye, she grabbed a mug and filled it with coffee and a splash of cream.

"I've slept better," he admitted.

Holly darted her eyes to his and he threw her a lopsided smile that had the distinct hint of…guilt.

Disappointment flooded Holly's chest and sunk her heart into the pit of her stomach. So he was regretting the kiss, then. She balled her fists at her sides to keep them from shaking. She should have known it was all too good to be true. That she had given her heart away too quickly. That she'd been fooled yet again. That she was silly for getting caught up in the romance of their circumstances, and the hope that Christmas still ironically brought her year after year.

"I'm sorry to hear that," she managed, her tone cool.

"You should be," he said. "Because it's your fault."

Holly frowned at the accusation and wrapped her hand around the coffee cup still on the counter. "How's that?" she asked.

Max shrugged and the corner of his lip tugged in amusement. "I could have slept better if I wasn't thinking about that kiss."

Holly's pressed her lips together so he couldn't see how much this pleased her. She searched his face in bewilderment. "I…I see," she stammered.

"Is it too much for a guy to hope that you might have been thinking about me, too?"

He met her gaze from under the hood of his lashes, his rugged face suddenly taken over by a vulnerable expression. Holly's nerves immediately dissolved and her insides flooded with warmth. "I didn't sleep much, either," she admitted.

"Guess we'll both be in need of a nap today, then," Max

said. His blue eyes twinkled mischievously in the sunlight that poured through the window.

Holly offered a noncommittal shrug as she watched him. "That might be nice."

The corner of his lip curled into a suggestive smile. He stepped toward her, reaching out a hand to skim her waist, and Holly shuddered back a surge of fresh heat at the pleasure the small gesture ignited.

"How about a little something to tide us over?" he asked, his voice husky with desire as he leaned into her.

Holly lifted her chin as her lips met his. His mouth was familiar now, his lips sweet to the taste. She ran her hands down his chest, feeling the soft wool of his sweater. As Max's strong hands cupped her hips she slid her hands higher up against the back of his neck, massaging the silky locks of his hair as she pressed her body close into his, her body throbbing with arousal and need.

Sensing her response, Max groaned into her mouth as his tongue continued its dance. Grazing his hands lower to clutch the back of her thighs, he lifted her effortlessly onto the counter, and she parted her knees to allow him to press closer against her. Their mouths were frantic now, insatiable in the pleasure the union of their lips could bring. Max slid his hands from her hips and pulled at the bottom of her shirt until his fingers were free to wander up her bare stomach. Holly shuddered at the sensation—a long, deep quiver that pulsed the insides of her thighs. She wrapped her legs tighter around Max's chiseled frame as his fingers splayed to caress her breast over the lace of her bra. He found the center and began to tease the bud with the tips of his fingers until Holly groaned and tore her lips from his mouth. She buried her face in the nape of his neck as he stroked her tender flesh and then slowly pulled back the flimsy fabric until his warm hand was smooth and soft against her skin.

Tilting her head, she accepted the spine-tingling graze of his mouth against the nape of her neck, clutching the broad strength of his shoulders against her as his fingers performed their magic.

Max sighed into her ear as her body shuddered against his. He slid his hand slowly down her stomach and glanced up from beneath his hooded brow. His cheeks were flushed and his eyes glazed as he met her heated stare. Holly's chest rose and fell with lingering desire and with a grin, she reached over and smoothed his hair.

Sliding off the counter, Holly ran a shaking hand through her own chestnut locks, her skin still quivering from Max's touch. "I suppose we should eat..." She glanced halfheartedly toward the stove.

"You certainly have a way of stirring up my appetite." Max grinned, lifting an eyebrow and Holly felt her insides melt. Turning to the stove, he lifted a lid off a saucepan and asked, "What's for breakfast? Mmm... French toast." He turned to her. "Why don't you let me serve you for a change?"

Holly smiled. "With pleasure, sir."

Max plated the food, then pulled a stool away from the counter and sat down, patting the chair next to him for her to join him. She couldn't remember the last time she had sat in her kitchen and enjoyed a meal. It was usually taken over by staff. Not that she minded, but she had to admit there was something deliciously casual about eating breakfast in this setting.

"Are you going back to the Christmas Market today?" Max asked as he cut into his food.

Holly took a gulp of coffee, trying to pull her mind away from the intensity of their embrace. "No, I sold out yesterday, actually. Five hundred dollars richer."

"Really?" Max raised a brow.

"Why do you sound so surprised?"

"Last I saw you were handing the jars away for free," he said with a shrug.

Holly stifled a smile and sipped at her coffee, unable to fully tear her mind from the experience of his touch. The sensation of his hands on her skin had only served to make her want more. She no longer had an appetite. Not for food, anyway. There was only one thing she had a taste for and it was Max's mouth pressed firmly on her own. Listlessly, she dragged her fork over the plate. Even the waft of cinnamon and vanilla couldn't entice her.

"Do you have more business in town today?"

Max paused. "Maybe. Depends how the day goes."

Holly nodded slowly, trying to comprehend. "You're almost finished with it, then?"

Max set down his fork and turned to her. "I'll actually be disappointed to leave," he said, his voice husky.

Then don't, Holly wanted to shout. Instead, she asked, "Will you still stay through Christmas?"

Max shifted his eyes. "That's the plan."

"And then back to New York," she stated sadly.

Max stirred in his seat and reached for his coffee mug. "Do you ever miss city life?"

Holly had considered the question herself many times over the years, and dozens more times in the past week. There were elements of city life that were inevitably attractive: the shopping, the excitement, the din of the crowds, the buzz of the traffic. There were times when life in this small town felt almost too quiet, but those times were fleeting and rare. She made sure of that.

"Occasionally," she answered honestly.

Beside her, Max's posture seemed to shift. "Do you get back to Boston often?"

"No," she said. "I haven't been back since I moved to Maple Woods."

Max appeared baffled, a line creasing his forehead. "Not even to visit your family?"

"Oh," Holly said. She hesitated, lowering her eyes and forcing a shy smile to cover the awkwardness she felt. "I don't have a family, actually. Not…anymore."

She lifted her gaze to Max. He was watching her with an unsurpassed intensity, his eyes flashing with shock. "I'm sorry. I didn't know."

"How could you?" she asked mildly, setting down her fork. She realized that all this time she had been suspicious of Max, sensing that he was being evasive and overly mysterious, when she herself had hardly been forthcoming.

He slid a large, heavy hand onto her knee. A tingle rushed the length of her spine and pulsed at her tailbone as he grazed his thumb over her thigh. "Can I ask what happened?"

Holly took a deep breath and held it there. "It's not—not something I've talked about in a long time, really."

Tears sprung to her eyes, hot and thick and precariously close to spilling over and turning her into a blubbering idiot. She forced them back. She couldn't fall apart again. Not now. There had to come a time when she could talk about this without getting choked up. Maybe this was the time.

"My parents died in a car accident six years ago," she said quickly.

"Oh, my God," Max whispered. His hand moved from her knee to grab her hand.

Even in the heat of her despair, she welcomed the warmth of his touch on her cold fingers. "It was…awful," she said shakily. "We were driving back to Boston, from Maple Woods, actually, and the car hit a patch of black ice."

Max leaned forward. "You were in the car?"

A knot had locked in Holly's throat. She nodded her response, unable to speak. If she permitted herself, she could still hear the squeal of the brakes, her mother's piercing scream, the devastating crunch of the metal. And then, almost worse, the silence. "I was in the backseat," she managed. "It was a frontal-impact collision. The car—it crashed into a guardrail. I got out with some bad bruises, but basically walked away without a scratch. Physically, at least."

Max rubbed his forehead, digesting this information. "And you've been on your own since then?"

Holly tipped her head to the side. "Well, I had my grandmother until she passed shortly after and left me this house."

"That's a lot of people to lose in such a short period of time."

Holly's mouth thinned. It definitely was.

"But you stayed in Boston after..."

"After my parents died?" Holly finished, sensing his unease. "I did. And I wish I hadn't."

"Why?"

"My priorities were in the wrong place. I should have moved here to be with my grandmother. I...I didn't realize she would be gone soon, too. I thought I had time, that life couldn't be so cruel.... I had this boyfriend, and I thought we had a future together. I thought I was moving on with my life, moving past the hurt, looking toward the next phase instead of holding on to the past. But...it turns out I was spending my time with the wrong person. I should have been here, with my grandmother." She gritted her teeth, thinking once again about how much she had sacrificed by pinning all her hopes on Brendan. If she had known he didn't see a future with her, she would have come back to Maple Woods and spent the last months of her grandmother's life at her side.

"Everyone has regrets, Holly," Max said.

Oh, she knew all about regrets. And that was why she was so determined not to make the same mistake twice. She had learned the hard way what it meant to give your heart to the wrong person. Life was too precious to waste on people who didn't truly care about you.

Maybe that was why she was so attached to Maple Woods and The White Barn Inn. Even if these people weren't her family, they cared about her. She knew they did.

"I know that you think it's a bit strange of me to get so enthusiastic about Christmas—"

"Oh, now. I wouldn't say that," Max objected.

She shot him a good-natured accusatory look and his cheeks colored with guilt. "Well, maybe I *have* hinted at that impression," he admitted. "But that wasn't entirely fair. Besides, it's quirky. And it…it made me want to get to know you."

Holly's heart leaped at his confession. Maybe he wasn't the Scrooge she had come to believe him to be.

"But what does all this have to do with your unbridled passion for Christmas?" he asked, and she appreciated his attempt to lighten the mood.

Despite herself, Holly grinned. Only Max could succeed in making her smile in times of sadness.

"That Christmas six years ago was the last day I can remember being really truly happy," she said. "We were here, in this house, and it was just so perfect. My mom and I made cookies, and my dad cut down the tree." She grew quiet, thinking back on that day, not knowing in that moment that everything was about to change forever. "The car accident happened the day after, on our way back to Boston. I guess that every year since I opened the inn I go a little overboard with the holiday, just to keep the memory of that day alive a little longer. This house is meant to come alive at Christmas."

Max squeezed her hand tighter and sat in companionable silence with her for a long time. When he spoke, his voice was hoarse with emotion. "I guess I'm not the only one with a family tragedy," he said.

He reached up and tucked a strand of loose hair behind her ear, his eyes closing softly as he bent toward her. Holly's pulse quickened as she leaned in to meet his lips with hers. She had longed for this moment since the second his lips had last left hers, and just as her mouth brushed his, a sharp clearing of a throat was heard from the doorway, jarring their lips apart.

Abruptly, Holly turned and with surprise said, "Abby."

"I've been trying to call you," Abby whispered urgently, clutching Holly's upper arm and dragging her through the dining room and into the lobby. "Haven't you been checking your phone?"

Holly craned her neck back to the dining room, eager to get back to Max who was still sitting in the kitchen eating. She felt trapped with sudden impatience. The heat of the moment they had just started to share was gone; breakfast wasn't the only thing getting cold since Abby's arrival.

"I'm sorry," Holly said, not feeling the least bit guilty. "But I've sort of been busy."

"With *him?*" Abby hissed, referring to Max.

Holly's eyes flew open at the insinuation. "Yes, with him. Who else?"

Abby tightened her arms across her chest. Her eyes blazed through Holly's. "Do you even know what you're getting yourself into here, Holly?"

Holly faltered. "Abby, where is this coming from? I thought you liked Max. You were practically pushing me onto him yesterday!"

"Well, that was before," she huffed.

"Before what?"

"Before I started thinking that something doesn't add up here."

Holly groaned. "Abby."

"I'm just saying, what do you even know about this guy?"

A lot, Holly wanted to say. *Enough.*

"He's a good guy," she settled on.

Abby's face creased with worry. "Are you sure?"

"Abby," Holly said sharply. "Where is this coming from?"

"I'm just worried about you."

Holly sighed. "I appreciate that, I do. But just yesterday you and Lucy were basically telling me I was being ridiculous for being so apprehensive. And now you're telling me the exact opposite."

"Okay," Abby said, taking a deep breath. She held Holly's gaze with hers and lowered her voice. "After I left the Christmas Market, I went to the grocery store to pick up a few things for dinner. And I ran into Max. He was talking to Mayor Pearson," she added meaningfully.

Holly searched her friend's face in confusion. "And?"

"They were in some really heated conversation. Speaking in low voices. It was really suspicious," Abby finished.

Holly stared deep into her friend's warm brown eyes. "And…did you hear anything?"

Abby crossed her arms and looked shiftily around the room. "Well, no."

"Abby!" Holly cried. She knew her friend's heart was in the right place, but already her resolve to give Max a chance was breaking down, wariness seeping in through the cracks.

"I'm sorry," Abby said. "Maybe I'm overreacting."

Holly's anger wavered. "No, I know you're just concerned." She paused. "Are you sure you didn't overhear anything?"

Abby's lips twisted. She stared at the ground, pensive. "I guess not. It just…it just seemed odd that they knew each other. I don't know…"

Holly shrugged dismissively. "It's a small town. And you know how friendly Mayor Pearson is. I'm sure he was just trying to be friendly."

But even as Holly spoke the words, she felt her stomach begin to twist.

Abby looked equally unconvinced. "It just seemed like more than that. Like they knew each other."

"Maybe they do," Holly said, throwing up her hands. "Max is here on business, after all. I guess it would make sense that he could have met the mayor." Holly's mind flitted to the library. The more she thought about it, the more convinced she was that Max's involvement here was tied to it.

Abby nodded. "I feel like an idiot."

"Don't." Holly pulled her friend in for a hug.

"So tell me," Abby whispered, a glint reappearing in her eyes. "Did I just interrupt something?"

"You did," Holly said ruefully.

"Then I should probably let you get back to it!" Abby gave her a sly smile and said, "I want every detail. Promise?"

Holly nodded and waved her friend away with false cheer. Standing halfway between the dining room and lobby, she had the deflating sensation that she wasn't going to be able to just get back to it. The moment was lost and Holly's old fears had returned stronger than ever.

"Everything okay with Abby?" Max asked in what he hoped was a breezy tone as Holly strolled back into the kitchen. His heart was still pounding, despite the smile in Holly's eyes. This was all happening faster than he had prepared himself for, even if he had set it into motion.

"Oh, yeah. She just forgot something the other day and I needed to help her find it," Holly said, refusing to meet his eye. She pulled the sticky French toast pan from the stovetop and placed it in the sink, filling it with water to soak. Max watched her silently, his gaze shifting down her spine, lingering on the curve of her waist before she abruptly turned to face him, her expression unreadable. He eyed her as she smoothed her sweater over her hips. A rush of heat filled him as he imagined his own hands following her slim curves.

Max's gut clenched as her eyes bored into his from beneath the shadow of her long lashes. He studied her carefully, trying to gauge what she knew. What Abby had told her. This was what he feared the most—that news would spread to Holly before he could come clean himself.

He couldn't wait any longer. He had to talk to her. Now.

"I have to ask… Do you really plan to run this inn for the rest of your life?" he asked.

Holly refilled both of their mugs with coffee and turned to face him. "I do," she said simply. "I don't think I would ever leave Maple Woods. My life is here now, in this house. It's where I'm supposed to be."

Max clenched his teeth. So there it was. So final. So official. He knew it. She wasn't going to leave on her own. And that meant he'd have to force her out. Out of her business. Out of her home.

And inevitably, out of his life.

"Even with all the sacrifices you mentioned?" he pressed. "Even though you never get time away, and you're always busy with your guests?"

Holly considered his question. "I like dealing with my

guests, meeting new people. I know what I want out of life and I guess I feel like right now, the closest I am to having it is by staying here, in my inn."

"And what is it you want, Holly?" he asked softly.

She tucked a loose strand of chestnut hair behind her ear, seeming to debate whether she should tell him. Finally she looked him square in the eye and said, "A family. A family of my own."

Max groaned inwardly. He should have known. A woman like Holly was looking for marriage. Kids. A house. Probably this house. He could never give her any of those things. All he could ever do was break her heart.

"Are those things that *you* want?" she asked, her eyes searching his.

Max looked at her and knew right then and there what he had to say. "No."

Holly visibly paled. The light disappeared from her eyes. "Because of work?"

Max shook his head. "I love my work. My work has filled my life with purpose. But that's not the reason."

"Then what is?"

"I don't believe in family," he said, realizing as he spoke the words that he had never articulated his feelings so concisely. *I don't believe in family.* Was it even true? For years he clung to this belief, but something about being here with Holly these past few days, confiding in her, listening to her, laughing with her, made him start to wonder.

Holly's jaw set. She folded her hands across her chest. "Well, that's really sad."

Max gave a casual shrug, feeling like a callous bastard. He could see the contempt in Holly's eyes, the hurt and pain he was causing her. It was better this way, he told himself. Better for him to end it like this, to let her go. It would make it easier when the truth came out. She wouldn't be so blindsided.

He wasn't the man she thought he was. Maybe he wasn't the man he'd led her to believe he was.

His chest tightened with realization. He wasn't the man he wanted to be, either.

"Holly—" His voice was firm, his heart was pounding. He was going to tell her. Now.

"I should probably go tend to some things," she interrupted coolly. "Let me know if you need anything." She refused to meet his eye as she pushed through the kitchen door, leaving it swinging in her wake.

For a long time after she left, Max sat stone-faced at the counter, staring out the window onto the serene landscape that, in a few months' time, would be paved with cement.

There was no alternative other than to give up all his plans and live happily ever after with Holly. And that was never going to happen.

The ringing of his cell phone pulled him from his rambling thoughts. With a skip of his pulse he retrieved it from his pocket. He recognized the number from the call display as George Miller's. And he knew before he even answered what the verdict would be.

Chapter Ten

Holly pressed her palms against her eyes as hot tears spilled down her face and soaked the white eyelet shams of her feather pillows.

She knew she had no right to cry. The warning signs were all there. She had seen them all along; it was everyone else who was telling her otherwise. But she wanted to give Max a chance. She wanted to have some hope. She wanted to believe.

What a fool she had been.

Finally dragging herself into a sitting position, Holly glanced at her watch. She had work to do to prepare for the New Year's guests, and she couldn't spend half the day crying over this man who she wouldn't ever see again after Christmas. Oh, if only he would leave sooner, she suddenly wished.

Holly crossed to her bathroom, splashed water on her face and ran a brush through her hair, trying to perk up, even though his words still haunted her. How callous could he be? To just shut down any chance of something they could have had only minutes after she had poured her heart out to him.

She never talked about her parents' death. To anyone! Sure, Abby knew. And Lucy and George. A handful of others, of course. But other than that, it was something she had locked in a box and tucked away somewhere deep inside her. It was easier that way, somehow. Not thinking about her painful past was her only way of plodding through each day and looking forward, not back. But then Max had gone and spilled his own story to her, and she felt so instantly bonded to him, so close in the trust he had put in her, that she had just reflexively done the same.

And the strange part was that it had felt *good* to talk to him about it. To let him see a side of her she didn't reveal very often, not merely the woman who smiled and charmed her guests every day as she worked at the inn. The real Holly.

The Holly he clearly had no desire to get to know any better.

She just didn't understand it. Why had he bothered being so open with her last night if he didn't feel something for her? She had known all along, of course, that he was only in town for a few days, that he wasn't here to change his entire life around, but the rest...

I don't believe in family. His words echoed again and again. It was worse than she had even thought. It was one thing to be married to your work like Brendan had been. But to keep the world at arm's reach—to be so cold and alienating—was entirely a different matter.

Holly lifted her chin and studied her reflection. If Max Hamilton thought he could waltz into town, have a little fun with her, and then waltz back out, he was sadly mistaken.

He had picked the wrong woman for that. Holly didn't do flings.

She believed in family.

Well, forget him, she decided.

Holly plucked a tube of lip gloss from a drawer and swiped it over her mouth, but it did little to help. Her eyes were swollen and glistening. Her cheeks blotchy and red. She realized that she hadn't seen herself like this in longer than she could remember. Not since...

Something in her stomach twisted. Maybe she wasn't the only one keeping people at arm's reach. It was the only way to keep from getting hurt. From going through this. She had protected herself for years from moments just like this, steeling herself from the possibility of more pain. In many ways, Max wasn't much different. Was it worth it?

Holly felt her anger subside. A strange calm came over her, leaving her with nothing but a heavy lump of sadness in her already aching heart.

With everything he had been through, could she really blame him for feeling the way he did?

She shook her head and flicked off the bathroom light. Regardless of his reasons, he was who he was. And Max was not a family man.

And that meant that he was not the man for her.

Keeping busy, Holly had learned, got her through the tough times, and today was no exception. She spent the morning organizing the activity list for New Year's Eve, and going over her receipts for the month. Max's car was gone, and before he had a chance to return, Holly decided to use the opportunity to visit Abby. The roads were manageable and she could use a friendly face right now.

Abby was already waiting on her front porch by the time Holly's snow tires ground to a halt on the shoveled driveway. She stood hugging her thick wool cardigan against her frame, her expression a mix of surprise, concern, and curiosity.

"This is a pleasant surprise," Abby said.

Holly forced a smile. "I'm sorry I didn't call first," she said.

"Oh, please. You know you don't need to bother with that." Abby folded an arm around Holly's shoulders and led her up the stairs to the porch and into the warm comfort of her cottage.

"I was just sitting by the window working on my knitting when I saw your car pull up," Abby said. She pulled the door closed behind them and guided Holly over to the couch. "Pete's at work so you don't need to worry about anyone interrupting. It's just us girls."

Holly sighed. "I'm sorry. You must be wondering what's going on."

"Let me guess," Abby said. "Is it Max?"

Holly looked around the room, wondering just why she had allowed herself to get this upset about someone she barely knew. But see, that was the thing. He had let her get close. After last night, she felt like she *did* know him.

Guess I was wrong, she thought bitterly.

"I was right about him after all," she said to Abby with a watery smile. "Or, maybe you were."

Abby's eyes narrowed. "What do you mean, I was right?"

"When you came and warned me this morning," Holly said.

"Did he say something to you about that? About his talk with the mayor, I mean?"

Holly shook her head. "No. I still don't know what that was all about."

Abby's face softened. She picked up a pair of bamboo

knitting needles and wrapped a strand of thick, hunter green wool around one tip. "Sorry," she said, lowering her eyes. "But I planned to make this sweater for Pete before Christmas and time is running out. I can't exactly work on it when he's home."

"Got any spare yarn?" Holly asked.

Abby handed her a ball of pink wool from her basket under the coffee table. She fished around for a spare pair of needles. "This will make you feel better," she said.

"Thanks," Holly said, managing a small smile. She randomly casted on a few stitches, the softness of the wool on her fingertips instantly soothing her frayed nerves.

"So what exactly happened?" Abby asked, glancing up from her project.

Holly shrugged. "It's just what I said. I was right about him all along. He doesn't want a relationship. He isn't that kind of guy."

Abby studied her. "But you only just met him. Maybe in time…"

Holly stopped her. She knew better than to reach for hope that wasn't there. "He was pretty clear about it. He has no intention of getting married."

Abby frowned. "He said that?"

Holly paused, recalling the exact hurtful, horrible words. "He didn't have to. He said he doesn't believe in family."

"What?" Abby gasped.

"That's what he said," Holly repeated. "I don't believe in family."

Abby's brown eyes widened, her knitting paused. "Wow," she said, lowering her gaze. She wrapped the yarn over the bamboo stick and pulled it through a few more times, shaking her head. "That's…"

"Horrible?" Holly finished. She gave a feeble smile when she met Abby's stare.

"Yes. Horrible." Abby furrowed her brow as she worked on the sweater. When she finished another row, she quietly set her knitting on her lap and looked at Holly. "But why would he say such a thing? There has to be a reason."

Holly gave a reluctant sigh. "Well, I suppose there is."

"Hold that thought," Abby announced, standing up. "I have a feeling we're in for a long chat and I don't know about you, but I need some hot chocolate. With a splash of something to take the edge off."

Holly managed her first real smile since Max's announcement and settled back against the chenille throw pillows while Abby disappeared into the kitchen. The couch was positioned against a large picture window looking out over the front stretch of lawn where Abby had stuck a plastic Santa and his reindeer.

"Tacky, aren't they? But I couldn't resist," Abby said as she came back into the room. She smiled out the window before handing Holly a steaming mug of cocoa generously heaped with whipped cream.

"Yum," Holly said, perking up.

"We were out of marshmallows. Sorry." Abby blew on her cocoa and then, deciding to let it sit and cool, returned it to the table. She curled her feet under her on the couch and said, "Okay, so tell me everything."

Holly hesitated. She sensed that Max's childhood was something he had harbored close and shared with few people. She frowned when she considered that he had felt comfortable opening up to her.

She gave Abby a brief recount of the past few days, leaving out the details of Max's past that he had trusted her with, and ending with Max's hardened proclamation.

"I just don't think he wants the same things that I do," Holly finished.

Abby pursed her lips. "But you like him, Holly, I know you do. Maybe there's still a chance."

Holly thought about this. "I don't think so," she said, shaking her head. Even that flicker of hope she had just felt was enough to remind her of how much she stood to lose. Max had stood his ground. Now it was time to move on.

Abby reached for her mug and took a slow sip. "Maybe he just needs time."

"No, I don't think that's it, either. He's been alone for a long time, you figure. I think he prefers it that way."

Abby shook her head. "What a shame. A man that looks like that…" She blew out a breath. "Seriously, though, all joking aside, I know that I was a little wary of him this morning, but he seems like a really nice guy from everything you've told me, Holly."

"I know!" Holly cried, desperation filling her chest. "That's what's so frustrating!"

"I still don't understand what led to this big statement on his part. What happened after I left? Did he just blurt out that he didn't want a family?"

Holly chuckled. "No. Of course not."

"Then what?" Abby asked, getting impatient.

Holly slumped against the pillows and skimmed her eyes over the room. "He was asking me what I wanted out of life, and so I asked him the same."

Was that how the conversation had begun? Holly chewed the corner of her lip. Somehow this didn't seem so dire when she said it aloud. "He asked if I intended to run the inn for the rest of my life."

Abby was looking at her with round eyes and a telling smile. "Let me guess? You said you did."

"Of course. Maple Woods is my home. You know how much that inn means to me"

"Would you be open to leaving Maple Woods if you

could have that family you want so much somewhere else?"
Abby asked shrewdly.

Holly already knew the answer and it terrified her more
than she wished it did. She loved Maple Woods. But if leaving meant she could have those things… "I want to get married. I want to have children. But I want to live in Maple
Woods. In my house. My family's house. It's all I have left."

Abby sighed. "I just don't want to see you throwing away
a good thing because you aren't ready to give up some of
your creature comforts."

"What do you mean?"

"I mean that you have been holed up in that inn for so
long that you don't even know how to get out there and
live a little. You are far too young to live like that, Holly,"
Abby said. "You've built this cozy little nest for yourself
and filled it with lots of strangers. But you haven't stopped
to open yourself up to something real. And lasting. So how
are you ever going to even find the one thing you really
want the most?"

The words stung, jolting her to reality. She knew it was
true. She knew what she had done. But she liked the safety
and comfort of the life she had created for herself. Perhaps
too much… "I should talk to him. We have had a few nice
days together. "

Abby nodded. "I think you should."

But something still remained true. "But he doesn't want
the things I do. He doesn't want a family, Abby. Not in
Maple Woods. Not in New York. Not anywhere."

"Maybe he felt rejected!" Abby said. She adjusted her
expression and muttered, "The male ego is a fragile thing,
Holly."

Holly wasn't persuaded. "No, it isn't his ego. I think it
has something to do with his own family." Her heart feel-

ing heavy as realization formed. "His own family hasn't been around in a long time. Maybe—"

"Maybe he's afraid of people leaving him? Of getting close?" Abby asked, raising an eyebrow. "My, my. Doesn't that sound familiar."

Holly gave her a dirty look.

"Where is he now?" Abby inquired.

Holly lifted her hands. "I have no idea. He's probably still working out his business dealings."

"He still hasn't told you any more about that?"

"No. Should he?"

Abby pinched her brows. "Huh."

"Abby!"

Abby burst out laughing and clapped a hand over her mouth. Her eyes widened in apology. "I'm sorry, Holly. I'm awful. I just can't help but think it's strange that he has all this urgent business in town three days before Christmas. In Maple Woods of all places."

Holly chuckled. "It is bizarre. I know. But it's harmless, I'm sure. He said he's in real estate."

"Real estate?" Abby repeated. "Well, that's boring."

"I know," Holly said wryly.

"And here I was hoping he was a federal agent or a fugitive or something. Well, I'm sure that I was overreacting about his conversation with Mayor Pearson, then." Abby sighed "Besides, whatever he does for business really doesn't have anything to do with you. It's two separate matters."

Holly realized she was right.

"Sit and stay a little longer. Calm down. Think about what you want to say. And then go back to that inn and talk to him before he's gone and it's too late."

Holly considered this tactic, and realized this is exactly

what she needed to hear. "I guess it can't hurt to talk to him once more."

"If he's anything like the guy I talked to yesterday, he probably feels terrible. He likes you, Holly. I know he does. And that's why I'm telling you that this one is worth fighting for. If he still walks away after you talk, then let him go. But not yet."

Holly nodded and picked back up her knitting needles. Not yet.

Max sat in his rental car outside Maple Woods's biggest pub, The Corner Tap, for over an hour after he had left the Millers' cottage. He left the car running to keep the heat blasting. The radio station crackled over the speakers. The reception was poor, but it was the only channel not playing Christmas carols, so he was willing to put up with a little static.

The signed contract sat beside him on the passenger seat, a quiet reminder of what he had done and what he was about to do. The Millers had agreed. George had signed. Lucy had been too tearful to do anything but hide in the bedroom. Bobby, at least, had been gone. At another friend's house, presumably.

Even though Max had once hoped they would sign, somehow now that they had, he was left with the burning wish that he had never approached them at all. That he had taken one look at Holly's sweet face and just let the whole matter of the property drop.

But he hadn't done that. And now it was only a matter of hours before Holly would learn the truth. The horrible, awful truth about why he had come to Maple Woods. And why he had stayed.

The Corner Tap. The lights flashed invitingly on the sign in the window. Inside he could see a heavy crowd, all merrily cheering and toasting, some wearing Santa hats, their faces illuminated by the multicolored strands of Christmas lights that framed the frosted windows.

His mind flashed once again to his father, who was probably sitting in a similar bar right this moment, buying rounds for people who didn't care about him with money he didn't have, and stumbling home at the end of the night to a dark, empty house. His wife, gone. His son, gone. Did he even miss them? Did he even care?

Max had done everything in his power to make sure that he paved his own way, creating a different path for himself that would take him as far from his childhood as possible. The misery of his youth had fueled him for years, giving him a sense of purpose and determination. But he was so busy running away he hadn't stopped to ask himself where he was going. Or where he wanted to end up. Or if he was happy.

He had thought he was happy. He had thought escape was enough. But these past few days with Holly had made him realize how much he was missing out on. How much more there was to life.

Shifting the car into gear, Max pressed his foot on the accelerator and swerved back onto Main Street, driving to The White Barn Inn as quickly as the icy roads would allow. He didn't know what she knew. He didn't know what she would say. All he knew was that he had to talk to Holly. Tonight.

It was dark by the time Holly stepped out of the car and glanced up at the top corner of the inn that housed the Green Room. While she was calmer now than she had been this morning, her mind was still at war with her heart.

She heaved a sigh, her breath escaping in a plume of steam against the cold night air, and trudged through the snow to the front door. She hadn't a clue if Max would be there or not, and her pulse quickened with the possibility that he had packed his bags and left for New York. After their exchange this morning, she wouldn't be surprised.

Almost gingerly, she turned the handle of the door. Holding her breath, she stepped into the foyer. The lobby was lit by the lamps and Christmas lights on automatic timers, but the inn was hushed. She craned for a sound of life somewhere, anywhere, and found it lacking.

With a heavy heart, she crossed to the front desk and hung her scarf and hat on the rack. She paused once more, listening for any sound of Max, but all she heard was the pounding of her own heart.

"You're back."

His deep voice cut through the silence. Holly jumped, and turned to face him. He stood in the door to the dining room, holding a few logs against his broad, sculpted chest. If he was uncomfortable with how things ended this morning, he gave no sign of it. The only reminder of their last words was the sad smile he offered as he walked to the fireplace and began tenting the logs.

"I thought maybe you had gone," Holly said softly, moving hesitantly away from the front desk. She couldn't peel her eyes from him as he went about starting the fire.

"Where would I go?" he asked. His back was still to her but she could hear the smile in his voice. He wasn't angry.

But then, maybe she was the one who should be angry.

"Back to New York," she suggested.

"Didn't you notice my car parked out front?" he turned and arched an eyebrow. Holly glanced out the window and saw his car in the lot to the side of the house. She'd been so distracted planning what she would say when she saw him she hadn't even bothered to register her surroundings as she drove up to the house. Realizing her folly, she managed a small smile. "Oh."

Max rolled back on his heels, having stoked the fire enough to get the flames roaring. He stood and turned to face her. "I had a meeting in town. Besides, I never would have just left without saying goodbye."

Relief washed over Holly as she let out a pent-up breath.

"It's good to see you," she said. The words gushed out and she realized how much she meant them.

Max gave her an apologetic smile. "It's good to see you, too."

He stepped toward her and she didn't pull back. Any earlier trepidation vanished as her body took over her mind's reasoning. He bent his head down to touch her lips, softly, almost hesitantly. But the emotion of the day had awakened something in her, and she pulled him against her aching body, willing him to claim her and finish things they had started that morning. As her lips became more demanding, she felt him return the favor, his kiss becoming aggressive and bold. She entwined her tongue with his and began running her fingers along the back of his neck, feeling the heat from his skin as he pressed her to his body until she could barely breathe.

Finally, he gently pushed himself back, looking into her searching eyes. She wanted to believe his kiss was full of unspoken words, that the things he had said this morning were untrue or said in hurt. His blue gaze was clouded, but the spark of desire was undeniable.

"I'm sorry if I upset you this morning," Max said heavily, as if relinquishing his own burden with the words. "It wasn't my intention."

"I'm sure it wasn't," Holly said. Hesitantly, she added, "But is that really how you feel?"

Max sighed and sat beside her. He raked his fingers

through his hair and studied the fire, avoiding eye contact. "The thing is, Holly, that there's still a lot you don't know about me."

"I know," Holly said simply. "There's still a lot you don't know about me, either. We've only just met."

Max turned and met her gaze. "Yeah, we only just have, haven't we? It's strange because somehow it feels like I'm closer to you than anyone else."

Holly smiled at the compliment and fought off the warm spark of hope that took hold of her bloodstream.

"I'm not used to letting people in," Max admitted. "Maybe I'm not very good at it."

Holly offered him a smile. "It takes time."

Max nodded, his brow furrowed. He hesitated long enough for her to sense that this might not turn into the happily-ever-after she had hoped it would be. That maybe he still meant what he had said this morning.

Max locked eyes with her and the intensity she saw in his gaze caused her breath to catch in her lungs. "I like you, Holly. A lot. And I don't want to hurt you."

Holly searched his face, unsure of what he was telling her, looking for an answer that wasn't there. She licked her lips, still tasting him. "I don't understand."

Max drew a breath. "Holly, there's something you need to know. Something that I think will change the way you feel. I…I don't even know how it got to this point."

Holly felt a flood of concern at his sudden loss for words. Her mind raced with possibilities as she watched his eyes darken and shift back to the fire.

Her heart was pounding. "Max? What is it?"

Max shook his head and swallowed hard. When she reached for his hand, he moved it away.

"Max. Please." She reached out to grab hold of his arm.

eliciting a quiver down her spine as her skin touched his. "Just tell me. What is it?"

The ring of her cell phone cut the tension. Holly felt a wave of irritation so strong it almost exceeded the relief she felt at its timing. On shaking legs she stood and walked to the front desk where she had set her phone, immediately recognizing the number on the screen.

"George, hi." Her voice was raspy and breathless from emotion.

"Holly, I hope I'm not catching you at a bad time." George Miller's voice was weary and she immediately recognized that something was wrong.

"Is everything okay, George?" she asked worriedly, her anguish over Max instantly replaced with fear. The roads were slick, it was already dusk. She gripped the phone tighter. When he didn't reply right away, she pressed, "Has something happened to Lucy or Bobby?"

"We're all fine," George explained. "But…"

Holly's stomach knotted. She barely managed to form her words. "What is it, George?"

"I don't know how to say this, Holly, but someone has made an offer on the land."

For a moment the room went still and all she could hear was the blood rushing in her head. She tried to make sense of what he was telling her and failed. "I—I don't understand," she finally said, grasping the corner of the desk for support.

"I'm sorry, Holly," George's voice was strained, tight with emotion.

Holly's mind fumbled through the fog. "I don't understand. What do you mean? What are you saying?"

"I'm sorry, Holly," George said again. "But I accepted the offer. I sold the land. It's…it's done, Holly. I'm sorry."

Chapter Eleven

Holly set the phone down and silently stared at the back of her hands as she pressed her palms flat against the rich surface of the front desk. They were her mother's hands. The same long fingers, the same small knuckles. The same curve of the thumb. The same hands that had held hers when she was little. And stroked her hair. And wiped her tears. They were so familiar. So constant and reassuring in their sameness.

The cool grain of the wood warmed under Holly's palms and she pulled back, dropping her hands at her side. She had thought it impossible to feel this way again, to feel so lost and alone and hopeless. This house was the only thing she had left of her family and her memories of them. And it was gone. Just like that. No longer hers. As sudden as that car crash that took her parents' lives. It was all just snatched out from under her, without any warning.

How could life be so cruel?

She had thought she was too old to feel this way. That nothing could replicate the loss of her parents. But standing there, staring at that phone that had so instantly shattered her world, Holly felt an emptiness that nothing could fill.

She let her gaze drift over the room, her mind bleary as she tried to comprehend the implications of George's words. Was none of this really hers anymore? But it was her *home*. The only home she had. Where would she go?

Max was standing now, across the room, staring at her. His face was lined with concern. She had forgotten about him.

"Oh, Max." She shook her head, trying to clear the fog. Her voice came out like a hoarse whisper. "I'm sorry…I've had some bad news."

Her eyes lowered once more to the desk. She didn't trust herself to walk. She didn't even know where she would go.

"Holly." Max's voice was soft, but firm.

She looked at him again, noting the ashen pallor of his cheeks. "I'm sorry, Max. I just… That was George Miller. My inn…" She trailed off, her mind reeling with the fresh hurt of George's words. He had sold the land. Sold her home, without even consulting her. In less than seventy-two hours it was supposed to be hers. For years she had been waiting for this Christmas. And now, suddenly, it was just gone.

How long had he been planning this?

A burst of anger erupted in her. Lucy. Lucy must have known all along and she had never even said a word! Not even hinted. Instead she had so callously told Holly how happy she was for her, knowing how important this was to her. Knowing what it meant to her. It wasn't just about keeping her business going. Forget the business. It was about preserving what was left of her family.

Holly's eyes blazed with hot tears as she looked wildly

around the room, seething with anger for people she had thought were her friends. Her mind spiraled as she wondered who else knew about this. Abby? Stephen? It was a small town and people talked. What a fool she had been to think anyone in this town cared about her. She had put too much faith in them.

"Holly." Max's tone was pained, the expression in his eyes pleading.

She looked at him expectantly then stopped. Her heart suddenly froze with awareness. "Holly. I am so, so sorry."

Holly's eyes widened as the reality of the situation took hold. He was in town for business. Real estate, he'd said. His anguished stare met hers, unblinking. It couldn't be, she told herself. Not Max. "No," she whispered, not ready to hear the words just yet.

"Holly."

"No." She shook her head, her gaze never leaving his, silently begging him to make this go away, willing his expression to change. For none of this to be true. "No. *No.*"

Max's lips pinched. His brow knitted as he shook her gaze from his. And she knew.

"No," she pleaded, her face crumbling in grief. The tears that had been forming spilled over, relentless in their fall, soaking her cheeks and dripping onto her sweater. She didn't even bother to brush them away or try and fight them.

"Please understand," Max said, his eyes holding hers. "I didn't know you owned the inn when I started this. If I had known…"

"What? What?" Holly insisted. "If you had known, you wouldn't have done it? You wouldn't have taken my home from me?"

Max shook his head, dropping his gaze, and Holly felt a fresh wave of frustration mount. She looked wildly around the room, desperate for someone to take this pain away.

But the only one there was the person who had brought it upon her.

"You wouldn't have done it!" she insisted.

Max looked up at her with a helpless shrug. "Maybe…"

Holly's heart sprang with hope. "Then take it back, Max. Take it back!"

Max shook his head, his eyes drooping with honesty before listlessly raising to meet hers. "I can't, Holly. It's too late."

"It's not too late!" Holly cried, her pitch becoming shrill in her frantic need to reverse the actions that had been set into motion. "The Millers will give you your money back. They know what this place means to me!" She lowered her voice to an urgent whisper. "Just take it back."

"Believe me when I say that I wished this could be different. But…it's business, Holly. It's not personal."

Holly's eyes flashed with fresh fury. "It's not personal?" she spat. "It's personal to *me,* Max!" she cried, her anger turning to despair as sobs racked her body. "It's personal to me."

She covered her eyes with her hands and cried deeply into her palms, feeling her shoulders shake violently. She felt nauseous. Dizzy and sick. Max reached out and placed a hand on her shoulder and she shook it off, glaring at him. "Don't touch me."

Max sighed and took a step back. He looked exhausted. Defeated. But it didn't bring her any solace.

"What are you going to do with it?" she asked quietly. "You're going to live in my house?"

Max's face whitened further. "George didn't tell you what the land will be used for?"

"No," she said cautiously.

Max heaved a sigh. "I'm a real estate developer, Holly. This land has been targeted for a shopping mall."

Holly gasped. Her tears momentarily ceased before silently welling again. "A mall?" she repeated, her voice so small it was barely audible even to her. "You mean, you're going to…tear it down? My *home?* For…a *mall?*"

Max's jaw twitched. He swallowed hard. "They might not even approve it, Holly," he said feebly, but his words were lost on her.

"A *mall?* That's why you were in town? That's why you were staying here? Meeting with the mayor?" She shook her head as the pieces of the puzzle fell into place. "Abby saw you. She warned me. I should have known…"

"I know how much this house means to you, Holly."

"No, you don't! You couldn't." Holly choked on a sob. "You don't *believe* in family. You said so yourself. You can't even *begin* to understand. This is all I have left!"

A silence filled the room and for one, heart-aching second Holly thought that maybe, just maybe he might change his mind.

"Please," Max said so softly she could barely him.

Holly swallowed hard, and looked him dead in the eye. Shaking with emotion, she narrowed her eyes at the man who had only a short while ago seemed so tender and kind. And perfect. "I *hate* you, Max Hamilton," she hissed, glaring at him through hot, blinding tears. "And I will *never* forgive you."

Max nodded slowly. "I'll leave."

"I think that's best," she said, and then turned on her heel and left him standing there alone.

December 23. She had been counting down the days all year, waiting for that sense of security, the comfort in knowing that her home was hers, that even though her family was gone, their memories could live on.

A soft tapping broke the silence of the room. Holly rolled

over in the strange bed to see Abby standing at the open door wrapped in a chenille robe. Soft light from the outside world was already peeking in through the blinds.

One day closer, she thought. The deed on the land expired on Christmas Eve.

"Thought I'd bring you some tea," Abby said quietly, coming inside to sit at the foot of the bed.

Holly pulled herself up to a sitting position and propped some pillows against the wrought-iron headboard. She sank back into them wearily, feeling drained and despondent.

"Thanks," she said, reaching for the hot mug.

Abby frowned, and patted her knee under the patchwork quilt. "How are you doing?"

Holly shook her head as tears threatened to form again, but never managed to surface. Her eyes were swollen and irritated, too dry for any further damage. "Not good," she mumbled, feeling every bit as miserable as she had since she first arrived at Abby's the night before. As much as a part of her wanted to stay in that house as long as she could, a greater part needed to be around someone that still cared about her.

"I figured as much, but I thought I'd ask just in case." Abby looked around the room, frowning. "I just still can't believe it."

"Tell me about it," Holly muttered bitterly, blowing on the steam rising from her mug.

"I just feel so guilty," Abby said, tightening her lips. She stared at a framed print on the wall, but her mind was clearly elsewhere.

"Don't feel bad," Holly said mildly. "It's not your fault."

"But I feel like it is in a way," Abby said, turning to face her. Dark circles had formed beneath her eyes. Holly realized with a sinking heart that Abby hadn't slept either. "First I pushed you on him, despite your apprehensions, and then I didn't listen to the little voice in my head that told me something was amiss."

"You did come and warn me," Holly reminded her.

"The way Max was talking to the mayor...something wasn't right. And instead of following through, I let it drop."

"Because I wanted you to," Holly said. "I wanted you to let it drop."

Abby held her gaze, unwilling to relinquish responsibility. "I should have known better," she chastised herself.

"Stop," Holly ordered gently. "You're a good friend. The best I could ask for. There is nothing you could have done differently. You did what you thought was best. Honestly."

Abby wasn't persuaded. "If you say so."

"I do," Holly said. "Besides, we both know who the real culprits are here."

Abby narrowed her eyes and fixed her gaze on the framed print once more. "When I think of the way that guy had us all fooled, it makes me sick."

Holly sipped her tea, which was sweetened with an almost overly generous amount of honey. She set it carefully down on the nightstand so as to not spill. "It isn't like Max acted alone, Abby. Lucy and George are just as responsible."

"I don't know who to be more upset with," Abby confessed. "Lucy has been such a dear friend to both of us. Why would she do this?"

"I've been asking myself the same thing," Holly said, suddenly feeling weary. No amount of scouring for answers was going to change the outcome or explain away the decision.

"Money," Abby commented bitterly.

"Probably."

Abby shifted on the bed, tucking a slippered foot up under her. "See, but that's what makes no sense!" she said, leaning in toward Holly. "You know the Millers don't care about getting rich. It doesn't add up."

Holly gave a listless shrug. "Does it matter why they did it?"

Abby's lips thinned. "I guess not."

They lapsed into silence, each consumed with confusion and misery, hurt and unanswered questions. It was Holly who finally broke the silence.

Thinking aloud, she said, "Max did say something interesting last night."

Abby peered at her sharply. "What was that?"

"He said the project still had to go before the planning committee."

"Huh."

For a fleeting moment, Holly felt her heart swell with a twinge of hope, only to feel it deflate just as quickly when reality came rushing in. "I guess it doesn't make a difference, though. Max bought the land. The Millers accepted the offer. Whether the mall gets built or not doesn't change anything. It is what it is."

"When is this planning committee meeting?" Abby asked.

Holly shrugged. "Who knows. But again, it doesn't matter."

Abby exhaled a breath. Her shoulders slumped. "Guess not."

"Do you mind if I stay here a little while longer?" Holly reached for her tea and choked down a sweet sip. It was the day before Christmas Eve, and that meant that tomorrow was her last real day in her home. It just didn't seem possible. "The thought of going back there right now...I can't bear it. It's too painful. If I went back it would just be harder to leave. Why prolong the inevitable?"

"Is he still there?" Abby voiced the same question Holly herself wondered.

"I told him to leave," Holly replied.

"Good." Abby's face was red with fury. "I can't even believe he had the nerve to stay at your inn, knowing what he had in store for it!" She clenched her jaw and grunted in disgust. "He has no heart."

Holly said nothing. A stir of unease rolled through her stomach. She reached once more for the tea, hoping the sweet honey would help, but it was no use. As much as she wanted to believe that Max had no heart, something deep within her knew it wasn't so. She had seen the pain in his eyes last night. She had seen the anguish and the guilt.

But then why did he do it?

She had thought their connection was real. He had felt it, too; she was sure of it. He wouldn't have opened up to her like that otherwise. He wouldn't have looked so help-less when she discovered the truth.

"He wanted to tell me," Holly thought aloud.

Abby turned to her, her expression impassive. "What do you mean?"

"He wanted to tell me. Last night, when I went back to the inn, he was trying to tell me something. And then George called."

Abby looked pained. "But why did he do it, Holly? Why string you along if he was planning this the entire time? Why be nice to you?"

"Why kiss me?" Holly added.

Abby shook her head. "Maybe he was really torn."

"Maybe," Holly said quietly. "But I guess it doesn't matter. In the end, he still decided to make the offer on the property. Knowing what it meant to me."

"In a way, that's worse."

Holly nodded slowly. "Yes. It really was."

But then, what else could she expect from someone who didn't believe in family?

Abby huffed out a breath. "I suppose I should go get showered. Are you going to rest a little longer?"

Holly nodded and pulled the quilt up tighter around her shoulders. She couldn't think about facing the day just yet. That required doing things and going places. She had nowhere to go. And nothing to do.

The inn. She hadn't even thought about it in the haze of her grief. The inn would have to be closed down. She would have to refund dozens of reservations.

"You stay here as long as you want," Abby said with a reassuring smile. "You'll get back on your feet again. Until then, our home is your home."

"Thanks," Holly said, managing a weak smile. She knew Abby was trying to be kind, but she couldn't ward off the ache in her chest. She loved Abby, and she was grateful to have a place to stay. But it wasn't the same.

She just wanted to be home for Christmas.

Max rubbed his eyes and looked at his watch. Somewhere during the night he had managed to fall asleep. He hadn't thought it possible with the way his mind was racing.

He knew he shouldn't be here. He should have left, as he said he would, but he couldn't. Not until Holly returned. Not until he had his final say with her.

Pulling himself off the couch where he had spent the night, he stumbled over to the massive fir tree and crouched down to inspect the gifts. His pulse quickened when he saw one labeled with his name.

Holly.

After a beat, he picked it up. The box was heavier than he had expected it to be somehow. There was a sturdy weight to it. On instinct, he shook it, feeling the hidden object shift slightly. He set the box back under the tree, smiling at himself for this childish indulgence before a sweet sadness crept in once more.

He couldn't remember the last time someone had given him a Christmas present. It was such a small, simple gesture. So very much like Holly to do.

Rolling back on his heels, Max stood and looked around the empty lobby. Only a few days ago the room had been buzzing and alive, filled with Christmas music and a pleasant buzz from the guests' cheerful conversation. Now the house was still and vacant. Everyone was gone, except for him. And he had no right being here.

Wasn't this exactly how the rest of his life had unfolded? He had built himself an empire, and he was living in it alone. The White Barn Inn was no different.

He had hoped that Holly would have come back during the night, and he had waited in the lobby for her. What he would say when he saw her, he didn't know. But he needed to see her. It was an all-consuming need. He couldn't let her go.

He pulled his phone from his pocket to call her and realized with a strange pang that he didn't even know her phone number. She was probably at Abby's house, but he didn't know where that was. He could ask someone in town, he supposed, but what would he even say when got there? There was nothing he could say that could take back what he did.

The memory of her parting words rang out, echoing in the empty corridors of this old mansion. She would never forgive him.

And why should she? He had taken the one thing that meant the most from her. He'd taken everything from her.

Max's stomach churned with self-loathing. Was this really who he was? The person he had become? He had tried so hard to better his life. To redeem his childhood. But this wasn't the man he had set out to be.

It took Max only fifteen minutes to get to the Millers' cottage. He took the icy porch stairs two at a time and tapped his knuckles firmly on the door. A tearful Lucy Miller pulled it open. Her brow creased when she saw him standing on her porch.

"I'm sorry to bother you, Lucy. Is George here?"

"He's at the diner," Lucy said, holding the door open wider so that he could enter.

Max stepped into the cramped living room. It was only his third time here, but already it felt familiar. The Millers were kind people, and it sickened him that he had dragged them into this.

"I need to speak with George, if possible."

Sensing the urgency in his tone, Lucy nodded solemnly. "I'll just call him," she said, ducking into the kitchen. From behind the thin wall, Max could hear her frantic whisper. "He's coming right over," she announced, reemerging. "Can I get you some coffee?"

Max managed a grateful smile. "Coffee would be great."

"I think I'll join you," she said. She disappeared once more before quickly returning with two mugs. "I didn't sleep a wink last night," she confessed, coming to sit across from him.

"That makes two of us then," he said, taking a hearty gulp. Adrenaline was pumping through his veins and the caffeine made him shaky.

A pounding of footsteps was heard quickly clambering up the porch stairs and the door swung open to reveal George Miller, his face creased with confused. "What's going on?" he demanded.

"Come sit down, George," Lucy quietly commanded.

She turned her attention back to Max. "My nerves can't take much more, Max. If you wouldn't mind telling us why you're here, I'd appreciate it. Has the planning committee already decided? Was all this for nothing?"

"No, it's not that." Max set the empty mug on the end table and leaned forward on his knees, feeling more clear-headed than he had in years, despite the lack of sleep. He stole a glance at the Millers, who were sitting side by side, clutching hands. Lucy's knuckles were white and her face colorless. Realizing they were waiting for him to explain, he cleared his throat. "I need to let you both know that I no longer plan to present the project to the planning committee."

The Millers turned to face each other. Max could see the mixture of panic and relief in their eyes. Before they could protest, he held up a hand. "I am a man of my word, believe it or not. I offered you a price for the land and I chose to back out. The money is still yours to keep."

The Millers exchanged another glance. Lucy nodded her head, silently communicating with her husband and George turned to meet Max's stare. "This wasn't an easy decision for my wife and me to make, Max. Lucy here has been crying for days over this. We agonized about selling this land to you, when we had already given our word to Holly Tate. She's our friend, and a member of this community."

"I understand that," Max said, his voice low.

"But the thing is…" George's voice failed him. He swallowed hard, collecting himself. "The thing is that Lucy and I have another responsibility that extends beyond Holly. And that's our son. And our town."

Max squinted, trying to follow their logic. He nodded for George to continue.

"I'm sure you've heard about the library fire," George said. "But what you probably don't know is that our son is responsible."

"It was an accident! He was smoking behind the library," Lucy interjected desperately.

A wave of shock slapped him, leaving him momentarily speechless as he struggled to comprehend the multiple layers of the Millers' situation. His expression, he knew, revealed his astonishment. "Does anyone else know?" he asked, trying to piece the facts together.

Lucy shook her head, lowering her gaze. "No. But it wouldn't have felt right to let it go. We...we needed to do something to set things right. But not at the expense of our son. He has an entire future ahead of him. I had dreams of him going to college in a couple of years! He's a smart boy...and we hoped he would get a football scholarship."

Max nodded. "You won't have any trouble sending him to college now," he said.

"We didn't know what we were going to do, but we knew we didn't want to keep this a secret forever. We kept thinking that if we could just pull the money together we could set it right... My father runs a construction business here, but he's not well and I'm afraid to burden him with this. We want to pay for it ourselves, to do the right thing, but the diner doesn't bring in enough. And when your offer came to us..." Lucy trailed off, swallowing back tears. "It was both a blessing and a curse."

"The money is still yours," Max reiterated. "You can send Bobby to college now. You don't have to worry about anyone finding out what happened."

"No," George said. "We're fair people. Honest. It might not seem like it, but we are. We'll go through with the sale of the land, Max. But we have a new condition."

Max sat and listened, first in awe, then in wonder, as the Millers detailed their wishes. When they had agreed to everything, Max stood to leave, feeling a hundred pounds lighter. It was time to go back to the inn, and time to let the Millers get back to their life.

"But, what will you do with the land?" Lucy asked as Max shrugged into his parka.

"I don't think I will do anything with it after all," he said.

Lucy followed him to the door, her brow pinched in thought. "Can I ask why?" she asked softly. She raised her eyes to meet his, searching his face in confusion.

Max gave her a small smile. "Holly has come to mean a great deal to me in the short time I've been here," he said. The words were true, but it felt foreign to be speaking them aloud.

Lucy beamed and reached out to touch his arm. "She has a way of doing that to people."

Max nodded and turned, walking down the stairs and back to his car, chuckling at the irony of the situation. He had spent his entire adult life pushing people away. How on earth did he end up falling in love with someone he had known for only a matter of days?

Chapter Twelve

As a child, Christmas Eve had always been Holly's favorite day of the year, even more so than Christmas Day. By noon on Christmas Day, the presents had been opened and excitement had peaked. But Christmas Eve was the epitome of anticipation and hope, of dreams yet to come true, of magic yet to be made.

But this year was different. There was nothing to look forward to now. No preparations to be made. This year it just felt like the beginning of the end.

Holly pulled onto the long drive and parked. Even though she'd been away for only two nights, it was the longest she had been away from the inn since she'd moved to Maple Woods. She stared at the property, already missing it, wondering if she would ever get used to being away from it.

It had been a long time since she had stopped to look at the old house from this distance. Sitting in the car at the edge of the estate, she felt almost in awe of its grandness of scale, its richness of history. She'd spent the first few days of December wrapping the posts in garland, carefully hanging a wreath on each of the windows and the front door. It didn't seem possible that somewhere in the near future, the house would be demolished and in its place would be a shopping mall of all things.

She shifted the gears and slowly crept up the drive, allowing her eyes to roam over the acreage. From the snow-covered blueberry bushes to the white barn far to the side, barely visible against the snow from this vantage point. She loved that barn—from its cheerful red doors to the weathervane standing proudly on the roof. Behind it was the pond, now frozen over for the winter. On a normal day, she would be down there skating, tracing figure eights into the ice. When she was a child, she and Abby would swim in the cool, murky water while her grandmother sat under an umbrella on an old plastic chair, flipping through fashion magazines and sipping sun tea.

Holly's heart tightened. She wondered what would happen to the pond. They'd probably fill it, pave it over.

As she finally neared the top of the drive, she couldn't help noticing Max's car was gone, and she felt strangely sad about it. The feeling was fleeting, but confusing in its effect on her. She was just disoriented and exhausted, she knew. She had gotten used to looking forward to seeing him and missing him when he wasn't there.

She pulled her car around to the back of the house and climbed out into the crisp air. A biting wind slapped at her cheeks and stung her eyes. Crunching through the snow to the front of the house for what would probably be the last time, she felt her heart sink further as her mind flitted back to Max. He had seemed so sincere! She'd thought she had softened his hardened heart. But maybe some hearts were just permanently damaged.

It would take her a while to remember that he wasn't the man she thought he was. That his advances had been nothing more than flirtatious banter, meant to cover his betrayal. That she had been duped, used.

Holly's pulse skipped as it did every time she came around to this sad, hard fact. No matter how much evidence was pointing to the contrary, something deep inside her still told her that her time with Max had been real and true. She'd seen it in his eyes, heard it in his laugh. Maybe he was this way with every woman he met, but her gut told her otherwise. Or maybe she was the one with an ulterior motive. Maybe she just wanted to see him so achingly badly because she knew in her heart that he was the one person who had the power to make this all go away. And she couldn't stop wishing he would.

The front door was locked to Holly's surprise—Max must have locked it when he left—so, after a bit of fumbling, she slid the key into the lock and turned the bolt. Already she felt like a stranger as she closed the door behind her. The house was empty, eerily still. Unlike it had ever been since she first converted it into an inn. Even during her slowest months, there was always the cheerful rumble of conversation from a handful of guests or members of staff.

The staff. Holly groaned as she realized the ripple effect of this horrible situation. She couldn't imagine a worse time than Christmas to let everyone know that they no longer had a job to return to, but she had been left with no other choice. She winced when she thought of Abby, who was so busy comforting her that she hadn't even bothered to indulge in the setback this had caused her personally.

A wave of shame took over when she thought of her oversight. When she got back to Abby's house, she would figure something out for her. A severance of some sort. It was the least she could do.

Holly moved quickly through the lobby, not bothering to linger. The longer she stayed in this house, the harder it would be to leave again. She didn't need to sit here and reminisce. There would be plenty of time for memories later. That was all she would have left soon. Memories and nothing more. At least those would be hers to cherish and keep forever—something Max or anyone else could never take from her.

Abby had been kind enough to offer to help her pack, but Holly knew it was better for her to do this on her own, despite how much of a toll the effort was taking on her broken spirit. She needed to do this at her own pace, with her own thoughts to keep her company, to have the closure she needed to be able to walk out of her house and shut that door behind her for the very last time.

Max gripped the steering wheel as he drove through town, recalling the dozens of terse emails he'd received from his senior staff, the confusion and anger he'd sensed in their voices during a conference call earlier that morning. People were upset, and understandably so. He'd told them a half-truth—that the site had slipped through, that it wouldn't work out. They didn't need details beyond that. It was his company, and he'd deal with the fallout. The anchors would be let down. It was possible several would act on their threats to pull out of underperforming centers. Hamilton Properties would take a major financial hit.

But it would be worth it.

He took a left and began to climb the long driveway to the inn. He held his breath, looking for any sign of Holly. He had spent another night sitting in the lobby, waiting for a sign of headlights, bracing himself for her return. He ached with a need to see her, speak to her. He needed to make things right, and he didn't want to wait any longer.

His tires chomped up the drive and he pulled to a stop. No car.

Max fought back the bitter taste that filled his mouth. There was still a chance to set things right; Holly would have to return to the inn eventually. It was her home, after all. She couldn't stay away forever.

By now he had resigned himself to letting her go, if that was what she wanted. He was used to people walking away from him; it was all he had ever known. If Holly was determined to never forgive him or see him again, that was her choice. He couldn't stop her.

But it wouldn't stop him from doing what he had to do.

Max turned off the ignition and stepped out into the chilly air. It was going to be a white Christmas this year— even the sun's rays couldn't cut through the cold. He pulled his collar up to shield his neck from the wind and darted to the front door of the lobby, fumbling in his pocket for the key. He hesitated, his brow furrowing in confusion when he realized the door was unlocked, even though he had made sure to lock it before going into town.

Holly.

He held his breath, his heart pounding as he quietly pushed open the door and stepped inside. With eerie calm he stood perfectly still, his eyes skimming the lobby, looking for any sign of her.

But all he was met with was silence.

Max inhaled deeply, and nodded to himself. He had set this into motion and now he was paying the price. It was time to leave The White Barn Inn once and for all.

But first, there was one last thing he needed to do.

It didn't take Holly long to pack up her clothes and toiletries. Her personal photos and mementos all fit neatly in a few brown packing boxes. She had fit her entire world into the bedroom, sitting room, and bathroom that constituted her living quarters. The rest of her home was open to the public; the door was always open for any passing stranger who wanted to enter her world, even for just one night.

She did want to keep some of the furniture, though. When she landed on her feet, she would need it to make her feel like she was home again. Abby had suggested she have an estate sale for the rest; she could use the money to start a new life for herself. Although, what that life would be, she didn't even know anymore.

Maple Woods no longer seemed the place for her. She couldn't bear the thought of driving through town and seeing a shopping mall on this very spot she now stood. It would kill her.

And even her friends... Abby and Pete and Stephen were dear, but some pain cut too deep and some towns were too small. She understood now why Max had left his childhood town behind and never looked back. It was time to do this with Maple Woods. She couldn't imagine ever facing the Millers again after this. Their smiles, their diner, all of it would just be a constant reminder of their betrayal and of her loss.

Holly had a sudden urge to hide. To run from her life and leave her memories packed up in the boxes at her feet. Maybe she *would* go back to Boston, where she could get a new job and get lost in the crowd. Or maybe she could get a job at a hotel in another city, someplace where no one would know her or her sad story or would have even heard of Maple Woods.

She sealed another box. It was almost time to leave. Dragging this out would only make things worse. Holly took one last look around the bedroom, feeling strangely detached and peaceful. It was too surreal to accept yet. Someday it would hit her, but not today. Not while this house still stood intact, at least. Not while she was still a part of it.

As much as she wanted to load up her car and drive away right then, before the inevitable flood of tears took hold, there was still business to be done. Holly smiled weakly to herself—she had taken such pride in making over this building as an inn and providing for her guests. She had run a tight ship, and she would still do so now, to the bitter end.

She wandered back through the corridors, growing dim in the fading sunlight, mentally forming a list of everything she would have to grab from the front desk, but stopped dead in her tracks when she saw the golden flames crackling in the fireplace at the far end of the room. Her heart wrenched, her chest heaving with each breath.

Max. He was still here.

"Max." Her voice caught the knot in her throat, barely coming out as a stifled whisper, its tone laced with hope she didn't even know was there.

She slowly put one foot in front of the other as she tiptoed further into the vast space, her eyes scanning for any sign of him. Gingerly, she crossed the room to the hearth, her eyes focusing on something else that hadn't been there just a short while ago.

She reached out to the mantel and touched the stocking that hung beside Abby's and the other members of the staff. The ones Abby had knitted and that Holly had hung so carefully. The stockings had been empty all this time, meant for nothing more than a decoration and eventually a small gift from the Secret Santa exchange they did every year and she knew at once that the gift tucked into her stocking was not from Abby or Stephen or any other member of the small group that ran The White Barn Inn.

It was from Max.

Holly sucked in a sharp breath and let her fingers graze

the creamy paper that was tucked inside the stocking, poking out from the top just enough to make it visible. She pulled it out slowly and held it in her hands, pondering the possibilities. The paper had been rolled into a scroll, tied with a scrap of twine that she now set on the mantel.

Unfolding the crisp paper, she was surprised by the length of the letter. Her trembling hands caused the paper to shake and she scanned the words quickly, barely absorbing them and then reading them over and over until her tears blurred her vision and dripped onto the ink, smearing his last words to her.

Max halted at the bottom of the stairs, his hand gripping the banister. Holly stood with her back to him, her dark hair pulled into a loose ponytail that flowed down her back, glistening in the light of the fire. She looked so small, standing there alone in the huge room. So innocent in a way that touched him deeply and seized his heart. She hadn't done anything to deserve this. All she had wanted was something that was rightfully hers all along. He'd had no business coming in and trying to steal that from her.

Sensing his presence, Holly suddenly turned. Her eyes locked with his, and even from this distance he could see her tears, and it made his heart ache to know that he had caused them.

"I thought you'd left," she said, staring at him as if he were a ghost.

"I should have, but I needed to see you one last time first. I needed to try to make things right." He watched her, his breath caught in his chest, not ready for this moment to be over. In this moment there was a still a chance, still hope and he clung to it.

"I read your letter," she said with a watery smile. She

ifted it in the air, the fire illuminating it from behind. "Is t official? The deed to the property is mine?"

Max nodded. "It was never mine to take in the first place."

Holly looked down at the letter that accompanied the deed and back to him. "I just don't understand. Why did you change your mind?"

"It's like I said in the letter. I know what this place means o you. I understand how it could never be replaced."

"No," Holly said. "It can't."

"I shouldn't have gone through with it in the first place, Holly," he apologized, coming closer to where she stood near the large hearth. "I had no business being here or involving you in this mess."

"You didn't know at first," Holly said, but her tone had a hard edge. She was still bruised. He wouldn't have expected otherwise.

"No, I didn't," he said. "I honestly thought I was coming here to make an offer to the owner of the inn. That it would be a clear-cut business arrangement and that everyone would walk away with what they wanted. When I learned of the situation, I didn't walk away. And I should have."

"It was business. You said so yourself."

Max shrugged. "I guess I just didn't realize that the project wasn't worth it until it was too late."

Holly lowered her gaze and stared at the letter in her hands. She ran her fingers over the formal deed to the land. Her eyes shot up to his. "Was it really important to you? The project?"

It was now or never, Max knew. He had fought so hard o build a safe world for himself—his business and nothing lse. Now it was time to fight for something else. Something that meant a great deal more to him than anything else ever had.

"None of it matters, Holly," he said, fighting to form the words, "if it costs me the one thing that has come to mean so much to me."

Holly's eyes held his, unblinking. "What's that?"

"You."

Holly looked down at the deed to the property that lay flat against the smeared ink of Max's letter. She clung to the paper, thinking it odd that something that could mean so much could be both so simple yet official in form.

The tenderness of his confession tore at her heartstrings.

She looked deep into his blue eyes, noticing the way they crinkled at the corners, the way a faint line had formed between his brows. He had opened his heart to her, and now it was up to her to step inside.

A memory of how deeply he had hurt her cut fresh. He had broken her trust, blindsided her when she had finally dared to let her guard down. And now he was standing here, telling her everything she wished to hear but didn't know if she could believe.

"Max—" she started and then stopped as her mind waged war on her heart.

"What is it? What more do I need to say? Just tell me what more I need to say to convince you that I will never hurt you again. I'll say anything, Holly."

Holly searched his eyes. "Tell me what you want, Max. Tell me what this is all for."

His eyes didn't waver from hers, and when he spoke, his voice was strong and clear. Certain. "I want this, Holly. I want your world. I want *you*." He gestured to the room, to the tree. "Being here this past week has made me realize how much I've chosen to miss out on. I thought it was bet er to keep to myself, but I was wrong." He paused, giving her a lazy smile. "I want the tree and the stockings and the small town where everyone knows your business. I want to live my life feeling the way I've felt every day that I've been here. I don't want to go back to the way it was before."

Holly beamed. "You don't have to," she said.

Max's smile widened. "You really mean it?"

"I've never been more sure of anything," she said as she took a step toward him. He leaned down toward her, his eyes never breaking their hold with her own, until the moment his lips finally touched hers. His kiss was light and tender at first, sending a tingle down her spine.

He wrapped his arms around her waist, pulling her to his hard chest. His fingers traced lower down her curves, drawing her in as his mouth claimed hers with more passion. Holly ran her hands over the nape of his neck, through his hair, feeling the urgent heat radiating from his body.

Barely breaking their kiss, he whispered in her ear, "I'll never betray you again, Holly." The delicate rush of his breath in her ear and the featherlight touch of his lips on her skin made her shiver with need and she wrapped her arms tighter across his wide chest, pulling him close.

They continued to kiss, their hands tracing the other's chest, hips, back, until step by step they were moving together in the direction of Holly's bedroom.

"I didn't think guests were allowed back here," Max teased.

Holly laughed, letting her lips linger softly on his. "There are exceptions to every rule."

They fell back onto her bed, and Holly let her head drop back as Max traced his mouth along the length of her neck. She sighed, barely believing life could transform so quickly.

His tongue traced her bottom lip, teasing her for more, and higher still, sending a warm current rushing through

her. She opened herself to his embrace as he pulled her
sweater free, and she quickly released him from his shirt
His chest was taut and firm, and the warmth of his skin on
hers made her ache for him to touch her more intimately.

Her nipples strained against the lace of her bra, and Max
slowly pulled the straps off her shoulders, one by one, before unhooking the clasp and lowering his mouth to her
breasts. His tongue circled each nipple softly as his fingers
traced over her stomach, her hips and the rim of her panties, teasing her with his touch.

Her hips lifted with anticipation. She raked her hands
through the silkiness of his hair and craned her neck to re-
capture his lips when his mouth met hers once more.

"I want you, Holly," he said, looking her in the eye.

She nodded, unable to speak as she looked deep into his
blue eyes, noticing for the first time the slight dusting of
freckles that covered the bridge of his nose, the flecks of
brown that surrounded his pupils.

She lay back against the pillow as Max's lips trailed
down her stomach, over her hips, his touch so light, yet
her body so achingly aware.

He pulled her jeans off, then slid her panties down her
legs. Kneeling before her, he released his belt, and he was
soon hovering above her in only his plaid boxers, and then
nothing at all.

She opened her mouth to his deep kiss as he sheathed
himself in a condom and then entered her in one long, slow
thrust. Easing back slowly, he pushed forward again until
their bodies found their rhythm, his mouth never leaving
hers until the end, when he groaned into her ear and col
lapsed against her chest.

They lay against the soft flannel sheets, which, as
Abby had observed earlier that week, had up until this
moment never seen anything more exciting than a ro

mance novel. Their bodies entwined, each lazily stroked the heat off the other's bare skin, sighing with happiness or possibly relief.

"You know," Max said eventually, "I think your Christmas spirit might be contagious. All this mistletoe has clouded my judgment."

Holly smiled to herself. "So you're looking forward to another day of festive activities, then?"

"Do you know what's even crazier than that?" he asked in a husky whisper, his lips curling into an irresistible grin as his blue eyes danced. "I love you, Holly Tate."

Holly smiled. "I love you, too."

Bright sunlight poured through open curtains, filling the bedroom with a golden warmth and stirring Holly from her slumber. She smiled as the memory of the night before came back to her, and she rolled over on the mattress to run her hands over Max's smooth skin.

It seemed like an eternity since she had first met Max, when really it had been only a week. A mere matter of days, and her whole world had been turned upside down. She almost had to chuckle, thinking of the events that had brought them to this perfect moment. She could still picture the look on Evelyn Adler's face when Max had appeared in the dining room for breakfast that first morning.

"What are you laughing about?" Max mumbled. His voice was muffled with sleep and his eyes remained closed, as if clinging to the remains of a fading dream.

"Nothing, really," Holly whispered. She traced her finger down the contours of his bare chest and again let her arm fall lazily around his waist as she sank down deep into the burrows of his warm body. "Just happy."

Holly felt the shift in Max's torso, the twist of his limbs. Rolling over to face her, he wrapped a strong, heavy arm over her waist. "Mmm," he murmured into her hair. "This is nice."

"It is," Holly managed to whisper as desire overwhelmed her senses and caused her insides to quiver.

A smile began to play at Max's lips as he slid his hand down the length of her thigh. Holly sighed ever so slightly as a surge of warmth filled her. "It's Christmas," he said, leaning down to skim her lips with his.

And it was. Christmas Day. The Christmas she had been anticipating for years was finally here. She had imagined it so many times over—what it would feel like to know her home was really and truly her own—but never could she have imagined she'd be sharing it with the man who had swept into town and nearly taken it from her.

"It's your first official Christmas in your home," Max said, roaming his blue eyes over her face. He pulled his hand from her hip and brushed a loose tendril of hair off her cheek. "Was there anything special you had in mind?"

"I think this will do just fine," Holly whispered, nestling into the smooth curve of his neck.

"Mmm," Max murmured as he wrapped both arms tightly around her waist. She could hear the smile in his voice, and her curiosity was piqued. "There's just one little surprise I hadn't mentioned…."

"What's that?" Holly lifted her gaze to his, her eyes wide in alarm when she saw the mirth dancing through his.

The sudden chime of the doorbell tore through the house, interrupting their moment and jolting Holly away from the warmth of the bed. She sat up, wrapping the sheet around herself as confusion mounted. The bell rang again and again, the sound echoing off the walls of the large house.

Holly's brow furrowed in confusion and her heart began to race as she turned warily to Max, who was laughing so hard he was clutching his stomach. "What in the world?" Holly demanded.

Max wiped at his eyes as another round of chimes began, and finally groaned as the remains of his laughter faded away, until a fresh round of ringing caused him to sputter once more.

Holly was on her feet, frantically pulling on a sweater and socks, her mind reeling with the possibilities of what could be going on, of who could be all but tearing down her front door. Had she forgotten about a guest? Surely they had all canceled. No one was scheduled to arrive until New Year's Eve…unless… "Max?"

She slid her eyes to him knowingly as her heart lurched with hope. Max sat up in bed, propped on an elbow, his hair tousled, his eyes warm. He nodded to her just once, and that was all it took.

"The Adlers," she said, releasing a sigh.

He grinned. "It wouldn't be Christmas for you without a house full of everyone you love the most."

Holly beamed. "Present company included."

Epilogue

The White Barn Inn really did come alive for Christmas. Max smiled as he walked into the warm kitchen, drinking in the fragrant air.

"Smells delicious," he said, stomping the snow off his boots. He'd never in a million years have thought he would hear himself say it, but it smelled like Christmas. And he liked that it did.

"Turkey will be ready in an hour," Stephen announced from his familiar post in front of the stove. His girlfriend stood behind the island, placing appetizers on a sterling silver platter, and Evelyn Adler was perched on a counter stool, arranging cookies on a tray. When she noticed Max, she plucked the biggest cookie from the tray and handed it to him, smiling.

"Don't tell me Stephen's put you to work!" Holly said to Evelyn as she swept into the room with a half-empty punch bowl. Max's pulse skipped at the sight of her. She seemed to have grown more beautiful overnight. Her eyes twinkled and her rosy lips were perpetually spread in a warm smile.

"It's not work, it's dinner!" Stephen countered. "And you're in charge of the wine."

Holly added more eggnog to the bowl and garnished it with a sprinkle of nutmeg, smiling brightly. Her expression changed when she saw the freshly chopped logs Max was holding to his chest. "What are those?" she asked, her voice an octave higher than usual.

"Wood for the fire. I thought I'd pitch in."

Holly's eyes blazed with mirth as she took in the jagged and splintered cuts of wood in his arms. She wagged a teasing finger. "I never want to hear you make fun of my stint as a waitress ever again."

Max grinned. "Deal."

As everyone trickled into the dining room and lobby, Holly finished up a few quick tasks in the kitchen, smiling as she listened to the laughter and conversation flowing through the rooms. She had lived in this house for five years, had spent plenty of holidays here as a child, yet this was her first *real* Christmas here. Oh, her guests were lovely, of course, but she had never realized how wonderful it was to be surrounded by the real people in her life for the holiday. In her real home.

Picking up the bowl of eggnog and balancing the cookie platter in her other hand, Holly walked into the lobby and set both items on the coffee table. A shiver of excitement zipped down her spine at the mere sight of Max who was now sitting in a club chair, chatting easily with Abby's husband Pete, looking very much at home. It was almost impossible to believe that this was the same man, who, only days before, had looked more uncomfortable and out of place in this house than any guest of hers ever had before.

"I had a feeling it would all work out," Abby said, coming to stand next to her.

Holly turned to her, unable to suppress the smile she had worn all day. "Sure, you did."

"I'm just so glad that it did," Abby mused. "But there's just one thing that still doesn't make any sense."

"What's that?" Holly pulled her stare from Max and turned to meet Abby's furrowed gaze.

"The Millers. Why'd they do it?"

Holly shifted in her shoes. Max had explained everything to her—including the fact that the Millers had refused to accept any money for the sale of the land. The money would serve as a donation only. After Holly's fury had faded, she had been left with an overwhelming sadness that Lucy had harbored this secret for so long, and that she hadn't trusted Holly enough to share it. To think that Bobby had been responsible for the destruction of the library, and that Lucy had kept the knowledge bottled inside this entire time...it broke Holly's heart to imagine the burden her friend had carried.

"They had their reasons," she said to Abby. "I understand now. And I've actually invited them here today before they visit Lucy's parents."

Abby peered at Holly for a long moment and eventually said, "Well, if you're at peace with it, then so am I."

"I am," Holly affirmed, nodding her head.

"Miss Tate," Evelyn said, squeezing her way in between the two friends. "I read the most interesting thing in this morning's paper."

"What's that, Mrs. Adler?" Holly looked down at her dearest guest, finding it still almost impossible to believe that she was even here. Just when she had thought her Christmas wish list was complete, she had opened the door this morning to find Evelyn and Nelson standing on her doorstep, demanding to know why on earth the door was locked.

Max was full of good surprises, Holly thought, feeling all warm and fuzzy again. Though she couldn't have wanted more than for her house to be filled with her own makeshift family for Christmas dinner, a part of her couldn't wait for everyone to leave so that she could be alone with Max again...

"They're going to begin rebuilding the library in the spring!" Evelyn recanted.

"Really?" Abby asked, disbelieving. "But how? I thought there wasn't enough funding."

"Apparently an anonymous donor has come forward," Evelyn remarked.

Abby's wide eyes darted to Holly's, but Holly refused to feed into the knowing stare. "I think I heard about that," was all she would comment and she left the two women to go and greet George and Lucy, who had just arrived.

"Holly." Lucy's eyes were bright and tearful, and Holly could see the toll the past few days had taken on her. With shaking hands, she thrust a white pie box into Holly's hands, saying, "Peppermint chocolate cream. I thought it seemed...festive."

Holly smiled and reached out a hand to grab Lucy's wrist. "It sounds perfect," she said.

Lucy exhaled in relief and blurted, "Please forgive me, Holly. Some things have happened, you see, and we...we didn't know what to do."

"Lucy, it's okay. Max told me everything."

Lucy sighed and her shoulders slumped with release. With pained eyes, she held Holly's gaze. "I'm so sorry."

"I just wish you had told me what was going on," Holly said quietly. "You could have confided in me. We're friends."

Lucy squeezed her eyes shut. "I don't think you know how much it means to me to hear you say that."

"You and George have been like family to me since I moved to Maple Woods. There's no need to discuss this anymore. It's over. We're just going to keep moving along." She nodded her head into the room and flashed Lucy a smile. "Now come on in and get some eggnog. Dinner's almost ready and I think Max wants to talk to you about some other business venture he has."

Lucy paled. "What now, Holly?"

Holly laughed. "What would you think about branching out with these?" she asked, holding up the pie box. "Now that Max is planning to stay in Maple Woods, he's looking for some new investment opportunities."

"Oh, is he, now?" From behind them Evelyn's voice chirped. Holly turned to her, trying to suppress her smile at the obvious glee in the woman's eyes. "Should I presume I'll be seeing Max again during future stays at the inn?"

Holly laughed softly. "I think that's a safe assumption, Mrs. Adler."

Evelyn's blue eyes gleamed. "This place just gets better and better."

Holly watched as Evelyn scurried off to find Nelson. Although they usually didn't exchange presents until after dinner, she couldn't wait any longer to give Max his gift.

"Come here," she said as she brushed past his chair.

"What is it?" he asked, sensing her need for privacy.

"You haven't opened your present yet," she said. She pointed to the tree and Max's eyes sparkled as he leaned down and picked up the small box with his name on it.

"Should I just open it here?" he asked.

Holly nodded as Max quickly shed the box of its wrapping paper and lifted the lid. His expression folded, first in confusion and then in recognition, and a warm glow filled her heart as his eyes met hers in a tender, knowing gaze. The red-and-black toy train looked small in his hands, but not in the least out of place.

"It's just the engine, but I couldn't let you go through life without that train," she said. "Even if it is about thirty years after you asked for it."

Max grinned. "Some things are worth waiting for," he said, leaning in to kiss her.

Holly wrapped her arms around his waist and snuggled into his chest, enjoying the weight of his arms around her shoulders, and the security they provided. She looked around the room at all the wonderful people that filled it and she smiled to herself. A week ago this house was an inn. Yesterday it was empty. And today, it was officially home.

* * * * *

A sneaky peek at next month...

Cherish™

ROMANCE TO MELT THE HEART EVERY TIME

My wish list for next month's titles...

In stores from 20th December 2013:

☐ The Final Falcon Says I Do – Lucy Gordon

& The Greek's Tiny Miracle – Rebecca Winters

☐ Happy New Year, Baby Fortune! – Leanne Banks

& Bound by a Baby – Kate Hardy

In stores from 3rd January 2014:

☐ The Man Behind the Mask – Barbara Wallace

& The Sheriff's Second Chance – Michelle Celmer

☐ English Girl in New York – Scarlet Wilson

& That Summer at the Shore – Callie Endicott

Available at WHSmith, Tesco, Asda, Eason, Amazon and Apple

Just can't wait?

Visit us Online

You can buy our books online a month before they hit the shops! **www.millsandboon.co.uk**

1213

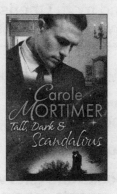

Join the Mills & Boon Book Clu

Want to read more **Cherish**™ books?
We're offering you **2 more** absolutely **FREE**

We'll also treat you to these fabulous extras:

-  **Exclusive offers and much more!**

- **FREE home delivery**

- **FREE books and gifts with our special rewards scheme**

Get your free books now!

visit www.millsandboon.co.uk/bookclub
or call Customer Relations on 020 8288 288